LOCKDOWN FANTASY #2

Compiled & Edited by

D. Kershaw | Maggie Pawsey | S.N. Graves

Also available and coming soon from Black Hare Press

DARK DRABBLES ANTHOLOGIES

WORLDS

ANGELS

MONSTERS

BEYOND

UNRAVEL

APOCALYPSE

LOVE

HATE

OCEANS

ANCIENTS

BHP WRITERS' GROUP SPECIAL EDITIONS

STORMING AREA 51

EERIE CHRISTMAS

BAD ROMANCE

TWENTY TWENTY

OTHER VOLUMES

DEEP SPACE

WHAT IF?

KEY TO THE KINGDOM

DEEP SEA

BEYOND THE REALM

Twitter: @BlackHarePress

Facebook: BlackHarePress

Website: www.BlackHarePress.com

LOCKDOWN FANTASY #2 title is
Copyright © 2020 Black Hare Press
First published in Australia in September 2020 by Black Hare
Press

The authors of the individual stories retain the copyright of the
works featured in this anthology

*All characters and events in this publication, other than those
clearly in the public domain, are fictitious and any resemblance
to real persons, living or dead, is purely coincidental.*

All rights reserved. No part of this production may be
reproduced, stored in a retrieval system, or transmitted, in any
form or by any means, electronic, mechanical, photocopying,
recording or otherwise, without the prior permission of the
publisher and copyright owner.

Paperback : ISBN 978-1-925809-87-9

Cover Design	Dawn Burdett	www.dmburdett.com
Formatting	Ben Thomas	www.blackharepress.com
Editing	D. Kershaw	www.blackharepress.com
	Maggie Pawsey	
	S.N. Graves	www.sngraves.com
Read Team	Alice Lam	www.alicelambooks.com
	David Green	davidgreenwritercom.wordpress.com
	Holley Cornetto	
	Jennifer Hatfield	jhatfieldauthor.wixsite.com/website
	Jodi Jensen	jodijensenwrites.wordpress.com
	Lyndsay Ellis-Holloway	authorlyndseyellisholloway.webador.co.uk
	Stacey Jaine McIntosh	www.staceyjainemcintosh.com

TABLE OF CONTENTS

WITH IT, HE GOES ON ALL FOURS

By Amber M. Simpson

The fire blazed beneath a pale, pregnant moon, casting malevolent shadows on the crouching shaman's face.

After years of studying the Witchery

Way, he would finally obtain the power he sought.

To assist him, he'd chosen his first-born, Yiska, for the boy's strength and stamina. Cheeks smeared with blood, the shaman chewed fervently, Yiska's flesh proving to be as tough as his spirit had been.

With a wolf pelt slung across his back, he stood and awaited the change. His bones snapped, his innards shifted, his eyes glowed fiery red—and the skinwalker loped into the woods, slobbering with anticipation.

FIFTH SUMMER

By Bec Lewis

The badly damaged journal of Sylvirah Oakbriar was found underneath an abandoned log-pile near Tunbridge Wells, Kent, in 1977. Only one page near the middle was legible. After many years' research, it was translated from the original

Sylvan language by local historian and dryad enthusiast, Mr Aiken Jones. At his request, we at Woodleigh Wonders E-zine are publishing this extract as a lasting tribute to Sylvirah.

***

Fifth Summer: My time is near. The babe within my belly kicks constantly, a mocking reminder of my restless nature. It is five summers since I left Hargate Forest, my home. I know Oak-By-The-Stream—my bond tree—still stands, or I would be dead already. Why was I, Sylvirah Oakbriar, so afflicted with wanderlust? Other dryads are content with their lot.

Grandoak will be angry when she sees

what has become of me, though she will have heard rumours by now, whispered from copse to copse across the land. We rival humans with our thirst for gossip.

Over-familiarity with human men folk is not permitted, and I have strayed.

A worse sin–I have acquired the humans' fondness for paper-marks. Instead of being lauded for putting our tongue in a more permanent written form—a rarity; usual attempts involve scratching lines on soft earth—I'll be reviled for daring to mark paper. They'll accuse me of marking my own kin. My sisters will shun me.

I may have to continue my wanderings once my travails have passed—if the ordeal does not fell me—but I will not abandon my babe. We will roam together until we find a place of welcome. But I so want to stay in Hargate. I finally understand the importance of family, of continuity, of stability.

If permitted, I will pass on my knowledge of paper-marks before my banishment, so that our kin and our way of life will be known through the ages to come.

I am but twenty hills from home now, and I am weary, but I long to see my forest before the end. Each step is more painful than the last, and I barely have energy to write. Yet I must continue the journal for the sake of history, and for my child. He will want to know his roots. If he survives (I sense it is a male) he will be called Aiken.

SEEDS

By Beth W. Patterson

My dearest one, I hope the prophet who transcribes these words will do so accurately and deliver them to you as swiftly as she may. I should have told you, while I was able, that you are the adopted daughter of Memory and Change. The world as you know it began in a fiery explosion, but the Transition came somewhat before, when we found you.

I was carrying Mnemo on my back as usual. We two were among the last of the First Ones, and even so I had held Mnemo in my arms when she was but a babe. But by then, she was a woman so old that her face was made of firelight, and her back made of stars. And still my hoof beats had never slowed after all these eons, my horns still carrying the four phases of the moon. The First Ones had been disappearing one by one, but questioning how or why was not in our intrinsic natures. Things simply *were*.

We had heard the detonation that day as we passed through the mighty infrastructure of flora and fauna, now called the Skotos Forest. The shock wave vibrated my bones and sent the trees bowing in submission. I did not know fear, for I am merely a function with form. And what I brought simply was what it was, for boon or for bane: change.

So we were compelled to investigate. The blast triggered an urgent reflex that launched us in the direction of this hell. I broke into a gallop even before Mnemo urged me onward with a kick. The pungent smell of charred wood and burned flesh grew thicker as we neared. Birds fled overhead, screaming bewilderment and darkening the sunlight with their numbers. As we came to a clearing, we saw the result of our existences, for painful Memory brings drastic Change. All that remained of the blackened hut were a few timbers poking out of the ground like broken ribs. A young woman, face twisted beyond recognition, was a hollow broken vessel, and beside her was a motionless little girl. Her little heartbeat was a polyrhythm to our own pulses, but whether she was unconscious or deliberately feigning death, we did not know.

The rustling in a nearby copse and the heavy sliding of rocks got our attention, and we froze at the sight of a gargantuan beast surveying the damage. Its mouth was pulled tightly into a satisfied saurian rictus, exposing teeth as long as a mortal man's forearm. Nose to tail, the behemoth was easily as long as two felled trees. We hadn't seen the likes of this creature in eons, certainly not before the dawning of human consciousness. But this was no prehistoric reptile. In spite of the familiar glistening black scales, short legs, and long serpentine body, it sported an array of features we found unusual: wickedly curved horns and a pair of stubby wings that flapped but were too small to bear it aloft.

The blue eyes deeply set into the shadowy sockets were unnaturally bright, eyes of a beast that had stared into the flames of hell for too long and gone mad with conviction.

Of course the monster did not see me, at least not in my true form. Other creatures simply lacked the ability to comprehend and retain the sight of a centaur with cloven hooves and two sets of horns, one set curving inward like a ram's, and one curving skyward like waxing and waning moons. If anyone saw me at all, they remembered something more mundane—Mnemo made sure of that—usually a gnarled tree that had an old man's face in the bark if they stared long enough, or perhaps they perceived a hollow in the side of a hill. My hoof beats were the music of the earth, and my tail could whisk away any shrouds of reality.

The hut had been completely torched with the sudden force of a lightning strike. And that's when we realised the strange monster was the culprit, as it coughed small jets of flame from its mouth. Mnemo filed into her records that this beast had been the first living thing to develop a bodily function strictly designed for ruin—but again, we did not know why.

Destruction is not a bad thing in and of itself, for it is often the road to creation, thus perpetuating the cycle. But we watched the giant lizard play with his fiery breath on trees, boulders, and outcroppings until it seemed satisfied with his power. We saw it regard the dead woman and orphaned child without emotion. They, too, had been no more than its target practice, not even prey. Something was inherently wrong with this creature, some urge to wilfully destroy. It swung its massive head around, pressed its tiny wings against its long back, and crawled away from the devastation, hissing in a deep voice, "They mocked me, and now I have work to do. No one will stand in the way of the dragon Dunatos and his Baneflame!"

Dunatos. So he had a name, and so did his kind: *dragon.*

As soon as his footsteps faded, the girl began to cry, the unnatural sound of innocence ripped away. Although my only function was to perpetuate the natural cycle of events, the tides had turned for me as well. I lowered myself on all four legs, knees and hocks in the ash, to gather her in my arms. Mnemo and I were natural causes made palpable, but even so, we could not endure the suffering of a little girl.

That's when I first looked into your dark eyes and knew that the world would never again be the same, for even Change changes. Because I was that Change, and now I had a daughter.

***

Delightful scapegrace, I loved you the instant I saw you. Wild and full of potential, you had a propensity for the absurd that no law of nature could explain. You simply accepted me and called me Meta. You did not regard my appearance as strange, nor did you seek my advice on wealth or power. You began to talk about mermaids, ghosts, haunted places, horses, and tribes of wild people. For only children cannot close their eyes to magic. I had seen mountains form and creatures evolve, but nothing was so wondrous as watching you turn a capricious cartwheel, your long dark tresses swirling like an erratic river current.

And so we took it upon ourselves to raise a mortal child. We comforted you as best we could in the wake of your trauma. The loss of your mother had left a scar across your heart. Sometimes you woke screaming from your dreams. We despaired, for Mnemo could not undo your memories, and I could not change what had already come to pass. But we held you and sang you lullabies of Earth's history. We had to learn how to provide food and clothing for you, for we ourselves had no need of either. We did not know how to raise you to become one of us, but we taught you what we knew.

Mnemo enjoyed you so. She taught

you numbers, stories, names of animals, and memory games. She explained to you how birds eventually came to fly, and what the wind says when it cries out at night for the moon. But in spite of your questions, she couldn't explain *why*. All knowledge had evolved in her subconscious, but she did not know cause and effect. And she wasn't expecting you to expand the tales, rewrite the rules, or invent games of your own.

The days of your training baffled me, frustrated me, and yet even as I fade from existence, I cherish the memories. Getting you to eat your parsnips or teaching you to properly swing a sword proved to be more difficult than coaxing continents to drift and glaciers to carve out the valleys. For only a nine-year-old girl can effectively negotiate with an immortal. You didn't need a sword—instead you had a unique style of rhetoric that only children possess and adults soon lose.

Your mother had raised you to be a hunter-gatherer, so you naturally excelled at using a bow and arrow. There was no such thing as childhood in those days, for young people were simply expected to pull their weight to the best of their abilities. We did not need food, but you were so proud of whatever quarry you felled or tubers you discovered that we shared your meals with pride. You were becoming well balanced between the sword, the arrow, and the art of logic, a hard worker for your scant years. Still, I delighted in instilling a sense of wonder in you.

I gave you a bag of seeds; the pouch was made of woven hairs from my tail. I told you about all things that constantly change. I showed you the lives and deaths of the animal kingdom, the moon and the tides, the cycle of seasons, and the sun's daily journey across the sky. But you wanted to know more. So I taught you how to plant the seeds and how burning a patch of land can clear it of weeds and make the soil richer for new growth. Then you wanted to know what you would do if there were more than enough crops, and I couldn't answer that.

We were Change and Memory. But you wanted to see Progress, and we did not know what that meant at the time, or even if there was a word for it. Yet by interacting with you, we began to evolve, and so did the minds of the people. They were becoming diverse in their natures. Some became nomadic, and some were beginning to settle. Tales were passed along through travel and trade, mutating into folkloric subspecies. Clearances for travel were widening into paths used over and over, and people had things to transport through mountains and forests to those who had no access to resources.

But as humanity began to expand, so did doubt and opposition. And as people began to fear the unknown, we felt a darker force grow stronger.

One summer afternoon we felt the ground shudder faintly and looked to the sky to see a plume of smoke barely visible in the distance. A long-bodied creature with clumsy fledgling wings rose for several terrifying seconds over the horizon before sinking heavily back to the ground. My spine, from the nape of my neck to my tailbones, began to prickle as I sensed his awareness of us. It could have only been Dunatos, gaining even more power—this time of flight—by way of destruction.

"Is that the same monster that killed my mama and burned my home?" Your question startled us. We had to evolve fast enough to protect you.

And so Memory became diverse, with Change expediting the process on four fleet hooves. I began to increase in speed, and Mnemo grew more complex. And as the god creates the mortal, the mortal creates the god.

***

"Why" was your favourite word, and for the first time we, too, began to question things. And after yet another night terror, you demanded to know the reason for the destruction caused by the dragon that had called himself Dunatos, and why he had wanted to create so much pain. I made a fire to bring you comfort, and as I held you and rocked you, we watched the insects dance with the sparks until your breathing became regular. Butterflies are praised for their delicate beauty, but it is the moths that like to play with fire.

Mnemo reflected on what she had seen of the giant lizard that had slithered away from the ruined hut. So we went down to the edge of a clear pool not far from our campsite. At the old woman's presence, the current became still, and although the stars overhead did not change, their reflections on the water swirled into images. Mnemo tapped into the monster's past and projected his memory onto the pool's mirror-like surface for all of us to see.

"You have to stay in the hut, boy. You are too sickly to go on the hunt. Make yourself useful, and help the women."

The words of his father cut him to the core. He may have been born small, but he was a male, and it was his right to join the men! He resented having to pound the grain into flour, to weave baskets. But if the women are gone, he thought, then the men would be forced to take me with them, for there would be nowhere else to place me.

He was angry. He would find a way to punish these females. It was their fault that he was not able to go on the hunt. It was his own mother's fault that he had been born weak and frail. Real men killed. His father had told him that killing was only necessary for food, but then again, his father had never paid much attention to the boy unless he needed to be disciplined. He would find a way to kill, and then one day everyone would have to do his bidding.

A quick blue lizard scuttling across the warm rocks caught his attention. The boy was quicker, though, and his swift hand pinned it to the rocks and scooped it into his clutches. Mouth gaping in defiance, the little creature writhed and fought in vain, and something stirred in Dunatos. He reached for a sharp stick, then thought better of it.

He stalked toward the village wise woman's hut and peered in. The decrepit old hag was so defenceless, stirring some herbs in an iron pot over the sacred fire. The boy's prey wriggled in his hand, but he did not release the lizard. He said, "Grandmother, give me the gift of transformation. This creature is small and weak, but if you would only give me his scales, his claws, his long body, I could be the most powerful hunter in the tribe!"

The old woman regarded him through rheumy eyes and sniffed derisively. "No good can ever come of that, Dunatos. Look at this pot. I am concocting a spell for strength. It is my secret to long life. I have wanted to share this with you since you were but a frail babe, but you first must show signs of compassion before I can give it to you, or else the spell will be tainted."

That traitor! he raged silently. She had known a way to make me strong this whole time! He grabbed the pot by the handle and swung it heavily against the wise woman's head. The sound of her skull cracking made him queasy, and she slumped over lifelessly into the flames. His world exploded in a blast of magic gone wrong, fire, and death. He was only aware of his body twisting and stretching, his weight almost too great to move. The hut became smaller and smaller—or was he getting bigger? His tail whipped from side to side, toppling the structure completely. He inhaled the flames that devoured the dead shaman's clothes and hair and huffed out a mighty pillar of flame...

Neither Mnemo nor I knew how to process what we had just seen, for we were not made to understand anger and cruelty. And you said nothing to enlighten us. You took one of the seeds from the bag I had made for you, dug a tiny hole in the ground, and buried it solemnly, a funerary rite for innocence. You whispered to the ground to be brave. You had become a natural sower of living things, of progress, and of hope.

***

Of course, we had to ensure that you were socialised. As we drifted from camp to camp, there were always other children for you to play with when you were not working and learning. Mnemo and I may have been wanderers because it had always been our incumbent duty to cross paths with mortals. But now we had twice the reason, even if the adults could not see us. You never insisted that your grown peers try, although you sometimes felt sorry for them because of their inability to wonder.

We knew that something had irrevocably shifted the day that one of the adults asked you, "Which child is your favourite playmate?" And you answered, "The little girl in the brown dress." To which the adult queried, "You mean the girl with no shoes? The poor one? Aren't you afraid she's going to take your things?"

You had new eyes after that. Some kinds of people looked different from others. Some had possessions, some had lodgings, and some slept in tents. You saw it for the first time, and so did we. It became imprinted in Memory. And now the populace was seeing it too, and some didn't like it.

We did not know how to respond to your questions as you agonised aloud over these new revelations. "Meta, why are some people different from others? Why do some of them look strange, and why is everybody unhappy about it? I could make everyone happy if I had Baneflame like Dunatos's and could make the different ones go away. But then some people would be sad! I will plant some seeds for the girl who has no shoes and wait to see what happens. Maybe something will grow and she will have enough." Waiting is hardest for a young child, and when you could not get answers in a timely manner, all we could do was wipe away your tears and share our meals with your playmate.

It was this very same barefooted little girl who came running to us as we were preparing to continue our endless journey, with cries of, "Need help! Monster take Gundo!" Gundo was her baby brother, and we were the only beings she saw fit to trust. Children could see us in our true forms, and the girl thought us no stranger than you did.

Mnemo cupped the girl's head in her gnarled hands, and the barefooted girl's panic subsided. The First One looked into the vast collective memory through the gateway of the child, like a fish slipping from river into ocean. She saw through the youngster's eyes a gigantic, terrifying animal, eyes like the blue centres of the hottest flames. He reached one taloned claw to scoop up this infant. He snarled at the girl, "Tell your imaginary friends Meta and Mnemo that if they want to spare this human child, they will find me in the village of Techni!" His wings, now fully developed, beat the open air until he slowly left the ground, the babe tucked against his chest. There was no doubt that this "monster" was indeed Dunatos.

Without your help as a go-between, we would not have known that there was trouble. Without your discovery of an invention called a "map," we never would have pinpointed the location of the trouble. We knew what we had to do. We dearly wished to spare you having to bear witness, but we had no choice.

***

"Where are we going, Meta? And what's a Tech-knee?" you asked astride me. "Is it like a part of your leg?" The paths were becoming increasingly clear as people were beginning to establish routes, and this freed your mind to find things to talk about.

I tried to think in finite terms before answering. Mnemo was riding behind you, but she wasn't contributing to the discussion today. "Techni," I explained at last, "is a developing community. People are beginning to find that if they live close together and get to know each other, they can work together and stay safer. Techni may become something even larger someday. In any case, Mnemo and I must face down Dunatos there."

"Why?"

"Because that's where he has gone."

"*No!* I mean…why do you have to face him down?"

I sighed, feeling suddenly laden with

the world as I carried you both on my back, physically effortless as it was.

"We used to stay out of the affairs of mortals, but since we have come to love a human, we can no longer stand aside and watch the world change for the worse. Dunatos is oppressing the people."

"What does that mean?"

"He is trying to make them do everything he says," I sighed.

"What keeps other people from *oppressing?*" you asked, trying out the word like a new pair of boots.

"I don't know," I replied. I had been using that phrase an awful lot since you came along, and I thought of my fellow First One named Sophia who had not been seen in eons. She could have imparted all knowledge to you, but I suspected that she was gone forever.

You said nothing after that, merely played with the little pouch of seeds I had given you. Mnemo braided your long, sable hair, and the rocking of my gait soothed you both as much as possible.

I reflected on the foundation of all people from all four corners of the world. They all had one common ancestor, which is thought. And now people were waking up and realising that they could direct their thoughts. But you had the extra concept of rhetoric. You had the power to influence people, and unlike us, you could be seen. We would need your help, whether we liked it or not.

***

The roads became easier than ever as my hooves found something else new: cobblestone paving. Night had fallen by the time we arrived in the collection of homesteads, fields, and public houses that were known as Techni. We came upon the masses that had not returned to their houses but were instead clustered together for comfort, holding torches but unsure what to do next. And the dragon stood in the centre of the crowd, holding court with bursts of flame from his maw. As Mnemo dismounted and helped you down, he snapped his fever-bright gaze in our direction.

I did not know until then that he could

see me. The people of Techni thought him either a god or a demon. I wondered what had made me visible to him until I saw what he was holding: a raw-boned baby, little Gundo. He was forcibly harnessing the pure energy of the child's innocence into his own vision, witnessing me through the child's eyes. And by subjugating one of the weak, he was making an example of those who defied him.

The people were beginning to see the differences among their races, and they were afraid. After all the diversity that we First Ones had created with so much love, one man was trying to put a stop to it all.

"There must be no more Change!" he roared. "The world is rapidly falling into entropy. You humans need a guardian. I will protect the people with my Baneflame, so long as they fight for my cause. Well, everyone except the women, of course. They are weak and emotional and can't be trusted."

He was clearly mad. He had been transformed into a powerful beast, but was trying to become immortal. He wanted to be deified himself, but it was just not possible. For even we First Ones were imperishable no longer.

But the people saw beyond his designs, for Dunatos could not stop the minds of the mortal community. They saw his Baneflame and saw potential. Such a power could be used for clearing fields for crops, for creating mines to retrieve ore and salt, for defence against invaders' attacks.

They all wanted its power for themselves. Some spoke of capturing Dunatos and enslaving him, but they were outnumbered by the fearful, who quickly threatened to turn against them.

He turned his mad gaze upon the three of us. "Come and meet my creation!" he challenged. "You will answer to Baneflame!"

He turned his head, dropped his jaw, and hurled a blast at Mnemo. The immediate curtain of fire threw his angular features into skeletal relief, a hideous caricature of himself. As the firestorm slammed into my companion, she exploded into a thousand stars, drifting upward like the twinkling fluff of a dandelion, to encode herself in the heavens.

Dunatos was still basking in the glory of his epic showdown. But he was not prepared for his haunted Memory, no longer archived by a First One, to return to him full force. For without her chronological filing, he had to suffer a lifetime of haunted memories in one cognitive eruption, and he crumpled to the ground, writhing like a giant worm in the sun. Only you and I knew what gripped him within, as the scenes replayed in his mind again and again. His roaring only whipped the crowd into a frenzy.

That was the first time the people had seen an incarnation of destructive magic. And the demolition of Mnemo, avatar of memory, was imprinted on their minds forever. Then he turned and locked eyes with you, and something primal stirred in me.

I had never felt terror until you came into my life, dear heart. Suddenly, I feared not for myself but for my inability to protect you. Something else wormed its way into me, something like ego. I could not flee the situation, not that I knew where I would have gone. I pawed the ground and drew my sword. I did not know why we had to fight to the death, but I did not question fate. Not even when he breathed his weapon at me, not even when I stared the final Change in the eye.

The adults only saw a frightened little girl and did not doubt the evil of their oppressor. They saw me as a giant boulder and that is exactly what I became then:

petrified and immobile without Mnemo, helpless against the burning firestorm of Dunatos. The last awareness of my body was that of shards flying, glowing cinders expanding to ignite tiny fires into every soul.

But unlike Mnemo, I had become solid stone, and the blast ricocheted back on Dunatos. As I transitioned into my nonphysical state, I watched his private demons consume him.

The mad moth had tried to harness the flame that lured him, but the Baneflame had backfired. The blast enveloped his body, too, killing not only his flesh but also his dark magic, the knowledge of which he had never shared. In one fell swoop, creation and destruction had called a stalemate.

Nothing remained but the sooty corpse of a tiny man, a shaken community, and a bewildered people needing guidance in their aggregate.

And that, dear heart, was the last that humanity saw of the First Ones. But the mortal folk no longer needed us in external form. They were beginning to tell their own stories. They were beginning to change for themselves what they wanted to change, and no longer needed us to shift the tides of their minds.

Would you destroy or create? In my nonphysical consciousness I could sense the crossroad of your mind and felt all that you had seen in your years, scant by my perspective. No matter what, there would always be fear and suffering, and it was the price to pay for diversity and experience. But you could do your part to instil kindness.

You were the one who reached out to them as the smoke was still clearing. You told them that ash was good for the soil and planted your seeds in what remained of me. Thinking of the future, you were the first to have Imagination.

***

Many battles will be fought, initiated by the power-hungry and the fearful. People will marry for love, for power, or for safety. People will be divided, reunited, and divided again, first by race, then ideology, commerce… In the end, it doesn't matter.

Aspects of consciousness and natural causes no longer need faces and form. Our work is done. People have since developed understanding, and so they carry us within them now. For energy can never be created or destroyed, only transformed. Mnemo wove her stories into every constellation above, endless tales for poets to decipher. And I became the Heartbeat of the Earth, to whom the shamans beat their drums. The magicians summon me to work their spells, and the lovers move to me and create new life.

Just call upon me, beloved. I am never far away.

THE AWAKENING

By D.M. Burdett

Ethereal lay in the darkened room, her eyes open, her brow furrowed in concentration, and her tiny hands clenched into fists.

Electricity fizzled through her bones as her mind focused on the mobile above her head, its colourful unicorns resting.

Her breathing harmonised with the energy in the air, and she felt a warmth penetrate her skin. A frightening pressure built up in her chest, the heaviness pushing her into the mattress. Her lip began to tremble, and a fat tear traced a line to her ear.

But then the mobile turned, and unicorns danced under dazzling lights.

Ethereal giggled.

THE SWAN'S REST

By Dale Parnell

It was March 25th, 1976, when I went public. I gave a statement, submitted myself for all manner of tests and examinations, I was even interviewed by a representative of the Prime Minister— apparently trying to establish whether I constituted a threat to the general public. As for the public themselves, they couldn't get enough of me and pretty soon they were queuing up around the block to shake my hand and have a photograph taken with me.

An immortal man living in a bedsit above a pub.

The Swan's Rest has been here for just over three hundred years, it's the oldest pub in the city. I helped build it, back when I worked as a carpenter, so I've always had a soft spot for the place. It has somehow managed to avoid any remodelling, so that apart from the television in the corner and an update to the electrical wiring, most of it is as it was the first day it opened.

In the early days, when I first started going there, it was about more than nostalgia. The place had always had a bit of a reputation—dim lighting and small alcoves of dark, almost black wooden furniture made it the ideal place for private dealings. I've seen a great many things change hands in those rooms, some of them of questionable legality. There was an anonymity to the place, which for someone like me also gave a sense of safety. Before I went public with what I am, I was convinced that if anyone found out about me, I would be hunted down and killed—either through fear or resentment. I always pictured a crazed mob chasing me down, demanding to know why I was so special, what right did I have to immortality? It took me a long time to realise that it's not about being special. It's not a gift or a blessing from God. It's a joke, a joke that everyone gets except me.

The first question everyone always asks is, 'how did it happen?' I've told a hundred different stories; magic potions, ancient curses, I even had one fool believing I had met a unicorn. The truth? I don't honestly know if I understand what the truth is. It wasn't like it was made clear to me what had happened—there was no flash of light or great, booming voice. It was more of a slow realisation, that after years of living I wasn't ageing the same as everyone else. My hair stayed brown, my back strong and straight, my eyes clear and focused. As everyone around me began to wilt and age, I remained the same. But it wasn't until I buried my wife and then my children that I knew for sure that I was different.

I travelled when I could. I feared discovery more than anything else and always moved on before people could grow suspicious. I've never taken another wife. There have been other women, a great many women, but I could not bear to bury another wife. That pain never quite heals.

I had been travelling for a long time, moving from place to place, ten years here, twenty there. I saw a lot of the world, and I watched it change, until finally I had had enough. I was tired, and all I wanted most of all was to go home. When I got into town and found that The Swan was still standing, it was as if it was meant to be. The landlord at the time—a tall, shaggy-haired bloke named John—agreed to rent me a room above the pub. Soon I was helping out downstairs, taking in deliveries and scrubbing down the flagstones at the end of the night. When the locals started asking questions I moved on, for a while at least, but I always ended up back here. I think John may have had some inkling that something was different about me, although he never said a word. But when he died, he left instructions in his will that my room be left vacant, and that anyone who could produce the key be allowed to stay and work the bar. The story became a local legend, but each subsequent landlord and landlady has always honoured the deal.

Lately I have been thinking a lot about the past. So much has happened that sometimes it's difficult to remember the details clearly. My mind is so full—people and places get muddled up—was I in Rome in 1850 or Paris? I remember a beautiful woman in a yellow dress, but can't recall if it was Rebecca in 1796, or Ruth in 1953? But lately a very specific memory has come back to me, stronger than any for a long, long time.

It is 1679. I don't know what year I was born, but I reckon I was around my mid-twenties at that time. I was playing cards, and it was late. There were four of us to begin with, old faces that hover just out of reach. And then a gentleman appeared. He was dressed finely, the buttons on his great, black coat gleamed in the gaslight. He dropped a heavy purse onto the table and was dealt into the game. He barely talked all evening, of that I am certain. His voice, when he eventually spoke, was like a treacle–smooth and sickly. I don't recall how the night played out, only that by the end it was just him and me—and the last hand to play. He laid down two sevens. I laid two jacks. The pot was mine, more money than I had ever seen, enough for a lifetime, or so I thought. The gentleman collected his coat and hat, and staring down at me he smiled–a cold, dead smile that flashed teeth for barely a moment. And then he was gone.

And so now, when the doors to the pub are pulled closed, and the few remaining drinkers sidle up to the bar to swap stories and tall tales, I tell them–I beat the devil at cards, and he damned me for it.

First published in *Bramble and other stories*, Dale Parnell, 2019

NOTHING BUT TROUBLE

By Gabriella Balcom

"*Listen,*" Nedira demanded. "I'm tired of having to repeat myself. You're supposed to *drink* from the veins, not rip them out."

Tilly shrugged. "Who cares as long as

I get what I need? If one dies, there are always more."

"All Saints' Eve is the only time we don't have to disguise ourselves, so quit advertising our presence. And, done correctly, the same humans can be used for years."

"Quit nagging. The old ways are stupid," Tilly sneered before walking away.

"She's nothing but trouble," Nedira told others. "Dead bodies draw attention."

Within moments, they'd drained all of Tilly's blood.

First published in *World of Myth Magazine*, 2019

THAT TIME THERE WAS A MINOTAUR IN THE GARAGE

By Joachim Heijndermans

"What...the hell...is that?" Carly asked, slowly and desperately trying her best to contain her rage as she stood in the driveway, staring at the astonishing sight of the colossal man with the head of a bull, rummaging through the tools and boxes that were stored in the garage. She was not succeeding.

"If I had to guess, I'd say that's a Minotaur," Garth answered.

"It can't be," Amy said.

"I'm fairly certain that the thing in our garage is a Minotaur, Amy," Garth scoffed, failing to avoid sounding snooty.

"I object to calling it a *thing*," Amy said. "It's dehumanising."

"Well, it's not really human, is it?" said Garth.

"Yeah, but we don't need to be mean about it," Amy shrugged.

"Then why don't we just call it the

Minotaur?"

"It's not a Minotaur," Amy said with determination.

"Amy, it's got the head of a bull and the body of a man—" Garth replied.

"Don't call it an *it*," Amy said.

"You just did," Garth pointed out.

"Okay, granted," Amy conceded. "I apologise. Call him a *he* or *Mr. Minotaur*."

"How do you know it's a guy?" asked Kimi, who just now joined the group to take a look at the creature in the garage. Not a moment after asking, the beast turned himself towards the four roommates staring at him. Kimi's eyes wandered below the creature's waist. "Oh, never mind. It's a *he*, all right," she said. "Should we cover him up? I don't want to get in trouble with the

Johannsens next door again. Their kids might see his...y'know."

"Who cares about the Johannsens! There's a goddamn Minotaur in our garage!" Carly shouted.

"It's not a Minotaur," Amy said again.

"Of course it is, Amy. Just look at it," Garth said again.

"I know what it looks like. But it can't be a Minotaur. This is Maryland," Amy said.

"And?" Garth asked, not getting her point.

"The Minotaur came from the island of Minos, in Greece. That's why it was the Minotaur. This ain't Greece, last I checked," Amy said.

"Oh," Garth mumbled. "You might

have a point there. So it's a *Mary*-taur?"

"A *Rocko*-taur? For Rockville?" Kimi suggested.

"That'll never catch on," Amy sighed. "And what if there's more of them? Like, all over the place, in different states? Won't that get confusing if we give each one a different name?" she asked.

"So wait, Taur is for Taurus, right? Taurus means bull, right?" asked Garth. "How about "Manotaur"? Man-bull? That'll always work."

"Ooh, I like that," Amy said. "Good job."

"Are you people done yet?" Carly snapped. "Look what that thing did to the garage door! Look at my car! Look at it!" she shrieked, pointing at the scratches in the paint job left by the creature's horns. One scratch was nearly as long as the car itself, stretching all the way from the hood to the gas cover.

"Again, not a thing. He's a he—" Garth began.

"I'll '*he*' you in the balls if you don't shut up!" Carly screamed. Garth crawled behind Kimi, hoping that the short girl would deter Carly from taking a swing at him.

It was then that the mythical beast bellowed out a cry of pain, following that by flinging a box at the roommates, who managed to duck away just in time. The box fell to pieces as it hit the pavement.

"I'm calling the cops," Carly said, grabbing her cell.

"Man, he nearly took our heads off with that," Garth mumbled.

"You think he's okay?" Kimi asked. "He sounds hurt."

"Oh, he's gonna be in a world of pain once the cops get here," Carly hissed angrily.

Amy moved closer, trying to get a better look at the creature. He slammed his human fists down on the hard concrete, nearly cracking it, so he was not lacking in strength. But on his hind leg, she could see gash of about seven inches long, with red blood seeping out and running down his brown fur.

"He's got a bad cut. Should we bandage him?" Amy asked.

"I don't think you should come near

him. He's likely to rip you to pieces," Kimi hissed.

"I'll be safe," Amy assured her, though not exactly sure how she'd pull that off. "Hey, fella. How'd you get in here?" she asked.

The man-bull grunted, and turned his back to her, rubbing his hand over the gash.

"You hurt? You hungry?" Amy asked. She then turned to Kimi. "Kim. You still got those sleep-aids your dad prescribed to you?"

"Yeah? Why?"

"We might need them for when we bring it into the house. Especially if we're gonna treat its cut."

"Are you sure we shouldn't let the cops handle this?" Garth asked. "I mean, it is a wild creature."

"He also might be the only one of his kind. You wanna see it shot and bleeding to death in the streets on the 6 o'clock news?"

Garth sighed. "No...I guess not."

"Ok, so we're gonna need those sleep-aids, Kimi."

"How are we gonna get him to eat them? They're kinda gross," Kimi said.

Amy thought about it. She suddenly snapped her fingers. "Got it!"

While they waited, Amy ran back into the house. Five minutes later she returned, carrying a selection of vegetables she'd raided from their fridge. To her surprise, Carly was still on the phone, waiting to be patched through.

"What'd you bring that out here for?"

Garth asked.

"I figured he might be hungry, so I just grabbed some stuff I thought he'd like. We can sneak the pills inside them."

"Aw, I was gonna make salads tonight," Kimi sighed.

"Are you sure he'd eat that?" Garth asked. "Didn't the Minotaur eat young maidens?"

"And young men," Amy added. "But c'mon. He's got the head of a cow. What are the odds he'll eat meat?"

"Bull," Garth corrected her. "He's got a bull's head."

"You should've gotten him some pants," Kimi said, her eyes still drifting down between the creature's legs.

"We'll get him some pants as soon as

he knows he can trust us. I'm hoping he'll come out if we feed him," Amy said. "After that, we can lure him into the—"

"Oh no! You are not letting that thing—" Carly snapped.

"Carly, I think he's just hungry and scared and—" Amy began.

"Oh! And that makes it okay to rip a hole in the garage door?" Carly snapped.

"Well, no. But—"

"Amy, we are not feeding that thing. We are not letting it into the house. And we're not gonna make it wear pants!"

"Then we should at least give it a robe. Seriously, you guys!" Kimi said.

"Carly, this isn't a raccoon that snuck into our garbage. He's half human, half animal—" Amy began.

"If he's part human, then he's trespassing. So, I'm calling the cops."

"They'll shoot him!" Amy protested.

"They're not gonna shoot him," Carly sighed.

"Oh, they're gonna shoot him," Kimi said. "And then two things will happen. Either they'll kill him, and then we'll be right in the middle of another police killing drama, or he's gonna go on a rampage throughout the city, and then they'll kill him once they sic the national guard on him."

"This isn't a movie," Carly scoffed, trying to stay calm.

"But you've gotta agree it could happen!"

"Ok, it might happen," Carly admitted.

"But we can't just let him rampage around in the garage like this. He'll total my car!"

Garth rejoined them, catching the last part of the conversation. "Don't forget that even if we don't call the cops, someone else just might."

"Right," Carly agreed. "So what's your plan then, Amy? What do you propose we do with the man-bull in the garage?" Carly asked Amy.

"Well," Amy began, still trying to think of an idea. "The woods are about an hour and a half from—"

"Noooope!" Carly cut her short. "We are not dragging that thing into the woods."

"Why not?" Amy asked. "We can get Garth's dad to lend us his pickup truck, put him in the back and drive him up to Glen

Echo park."

"Wouldn't it be better if we brought him to Virginia? No chance he'll find his way back here," Garth suggested.

"Go all the way to Virginia? That's a two-hour drive!" Carly protested.

"Also, Virginia? Eww," Kimi groaned.

"And what if we get pulled over by the cops? How are you gonna explain the bull-headed monster in the back?" Carly added.

"Also, now that I think about it, I don't think my dad would be okay with us driving a wild Manotaur all the way to Virginia in the back of his truck," Garth added.

"We'll put a tarp over him. They're not gonna pull us over if they can't see him," Amy said. "And if your dad asks, we'll just tell him we're taking the truck out for a camping trip."

"Camping? We never go camping," Kimi laughed.

"People our age usually go camping out of the blue. It's perfectly normal."

"But we're not actually going camping, right?" Kimi asked.

"Fuck no," Amy scoffed, shuddering at the mere thought of being outdoors, without a toilet and scared shitless at every noise in the night. And with her luck, her period would start at the worst possible moment.

"So you want me to lie to my dad? My own flesh and blood?" Garth said, gasping and sounding wounded, channelling his amateur theatre days.

"Obviously," Amy said. "Is that gonna

be a problem?"

"No," Garth shrugged. "I'll go call him," he said, retreating to do just that.

"Great! Now, all we need is a tarp and—" Amy began before Carly interrupted her again.

"And what, Amy? How the hell are you gonna get that thing onto the pickup truck and under the tarp? What is the great plan you have for us?"

"You don't need to yell," Amy said, folding her arms and sternly raising the ends of her eyebrows upward. "I have a plan, so if you'll let me, I can get into it, 'kay?"

Carly sighed. "I'm sorry. I didn't mean…... It's just that thing wrecked my car. My mom's old car. I loved that car. How am I gonna explain this to the insurance company?"

"Just say got impacted sideways by a bull," Kimi suggested.

"In our garage?"

"It was a lock-picking bull?" Kimi added, shrugging as if it would make the fib more believable.

"The damage isn't too bad," Amy said, peering into the garage. "Your paint is all scratched up, and you've got a cracked headlight, but I'm sure Garth's dad might be able to help you with that. We'll just take it to his car shop, and we'll all chip in for the repairs, all right?" Amy said, putting her hand on Carly's shoulder. "All we need to worry about now is getting the Manotaur out of the garage and out of sight."

"Where do we put him?" Carly asked.

"The yard?" Kimi suggested.

"No, the neighbours will see him," Amy sighed. "How about the room behind the kitchen?"

"Where we leave the garbage?" Kimi asked.

"Why not? The worst he'll do is throw some trash around. We can clean that up."

"That still doesn't solve the problem of getting him onto Garth's dad's truck," Carly said.

"We can worry about that later. I have an idea for it, but for now, we should just focus on getting him inside the house," Amy said.

"How do we do that?" Carly asked. "Are we gonna throw a lasso around his neck and corral him?"

"Oh, that would be cool," Garth said, having rejoined the group.

"No, Garth. No, it wouldn't," Amy sighed, already picturing her roommate being flung around by the giant man-bull, holding onto the rope for his dear life like a clumsy rodeo act. "We'll lure him with food. Get him to follow us inside the house and then lock him in the room behind the kitchen. It's not like we've got anything important stored in there, so there's nothing to break."

"Should we still try to tie a rope around his neck? Pull him along?" Carly suggested.

"Yes!" Garth cried out excitedly.

"No, Garth," Kimi groaned.

"It can't hurt to try," Amy said, shrugging her shoulders.

"I'll get a rope," Garth said, running toward the house. "You start giving it food and getting it to trust you."

"I'll get a towel," Kimi said, following after Carly.

"A towel?" Amy asked.

"Duh! Cover him up. Massive schlong, yo!"

"Are you sure about this plan?" Carly asked, biting her lower lip in a way that did not echo confidence.

"Yeah, trust me," Amy said self-assuredly. "This is gonna work!"

***

"Well, that was a terrible fucking plan!" Carly yelled, slamming her fist down on the kitchen table.

"It worked, didn't it?" Amy snapped back.

"And I don't think anyone saw us," Kimi whispered, peering through the blinds. A few neighbours gathered around their house, having taken notice of the massive hole in their garage door. Some of them were asking if anyone knew where those noises from earlier could've come from.

"I can't believe he cracked the back room door in half," Kimi muttered.

"Sorry about your desk, Carly. And your car. I'm sure my dad can help you get that mirror put back on. Maybe even knock the dents out of the hood and the doors," Garth said, trying his best to calm the situation and avoid an actual fist fight from breaking out.

"Can your dad fix the massive holes in the door?" Carly snapped at Garth, pointing at the chunks of wood scattered all over the kitchen floor and the two inch crack in the door, from which an angry bull's eye peered through every so often, as its owner grunted angrily at the four in the kitchen from the other side. The sleep-aid laced apples seemed to finally calm him down.

"In retrospect, it might've been better if we just left him in the garage," Garth said, nearly jumping a few feet back when Carly threw him a look of pure unsheathed rage. He shrugged and said, "Hindsight's twenty-twenty, I guess?"

"I'll hindsight you!" she shouted, flinging herself towards Garth and grabbing him by his collar.

"Whoa! Carly! Calm down," Amy shouted. "Carly, we'll take care of this. Garth is gonna go out and get his dad's pickup and a tarp. Then we can all drive the Manotaur out to Virginia," said Amy, hoping that Carly would calm down. She didn't.

"I want that thing out of the house! I mean it," yelled Carly. "Or I'm gonna shoot it myself!"

"With what? You don't have a gun," Garth laughed. The look Carly shot at him, a cold look of fury with the slight hint of a grin, shut him up immediately, and he gulped loudly from the implication. "Right? Car? Right?"

"Don't worry," Kimi chuckled. "We'll

have Manny out of our hair in no time."

"Manny?" Carly snapped. "You named it?"

Kimi said nothing. She just stared at Carly, trying not to crack. With a guilty tone, she lied: "Noooooooo...?"

"Dammit! You named it. Now you'll try to get us to go visit it every week out in the woods, and he'll follow us home and wreck my fucking car again!" Carly yelped, being on the verge of tears.

She began to gasp, trying to find the words to finish her sentence as she cried. Amy grabbed her and held her close, rocking Carly's head back and forth, trying to calm her hysterical roommate down. "Shhh. Don't worry. Once he's gone, he'll never come back. Just calm down," said Amy.

"I-I just...my car-and..." Carly stammered. The rest joined in the hug, holding Carly close.

"Listen, how about Garth gets his ass moving," Amy suggested, throwing Garth a look that screamed *get your ass moving*. "The pills are working. I'm sure he'll get sluggish in a bit, so he won't be too difficult when we move him onto the pickup. Then we can be on our way and drop him off in the woods. No more Manotaur to wreck any more of your car. Sounds good?" asked Amy.

Carly nodded yes. "Okay then. It's settled. Let's get a move on. And this time, no fuck ups, okay?"

***

"Okay, we didn't fuck up as much as before. Too bad he wasn't as out of it as we hoped," said Amy. "Still, we got him.

Silver linings and all?"

No-one replied. Carly grumbled something incoherent, while Garth was desperately trying to figure out how he was gonna explain the two horn-sized holes in the passenger side door to his dad. Or the dents on the rear made by bull hooves. He wondered whether, on the odd chance his dad did believe whatever story he managed to concoct, if he could run fast enough before his father killed him. Kimi was quietly mourning her favourite jacket, which Manny had chosen to devour in lieu over the trail of apples she had laid out for him. At least by eating her jacket, he inadvertently ate the spare sleep-aids that Kimi had put in her pocket, or getting him onto the truck would have been impossible.

Even though her joke fell flat, Amy concentrated her efforts on trying to keep the group together, though she was still shaken herself after "Manny" had thrown a thick glob of what she had decided to believe was mud in her hair, knowing full well that it most likely wasn't. She was pleased that she actually managed to get close enough to him to soak his wound with iodine and disinfectant, but she hoped the lingering smell would come out of her hair at some point. The beast-man himself was sound asleep, with only his horns sticking out through the tarp to betray his presence.

"Hey, how about when we drop him

off, we'll all go out to eat?" Amy suggested. "My treat."

"What's good around here?" Garth asked.

"I dunno," shrugged Amy. "I'm sure there's an Arby's or something around."

All those present in the car made a face of disgust. "I'm not that hungry just yet," Garth groaned.

"If the lint in my pocket can't hold me over, I'll say yes to Arby's," said Kimi.

"You're just full of great ideas today, Amy," Carly grunted. "Unless the guys at Arby's are up for grilling that thing in the back."

"No one's gonna put Manny on any grill," Kimi snapped.

Garth smirked and said, "Now serving:

Manny, the man-o-burger. It's a-*maze-ing!*" he grinned, doing a mental rimshot.

Kimi and Amy groaned at the awful pun. But then, one voice that hadn't exhibited the slightest tone of cheer that whole day, began to chuckle. To their surprise, it was Carly who was laughing full-heartedly, slapping her knee and gasping for air.

"I appreciate it Car, but it wasn't that funny," Garth said.

"No, it wasn't," she said between her gasping. "But the thing...and throwing at Amy...and Garth's dad's car...I...I can't breathe!"

Amy tried to give an angry look, or at least keep her composure. However, when she saw Carly laughing, she couldn't help but laugh too. Garth and Kimi laughed as well. The absurdity of their day was just too much for them. By the time they all calmed down, they were close to their exit.

***

They parked the car not too far from the edge of the park. Kimi was sitting in the back of the van by the sleeping man-beast, gently rubbing his coarse fur. "Don't worry, buddy. You'll soon be back where you belong."

"The Appalachian trail?" Amy asked. "I'm don't think it's known for its man-bull population."

"Wouldn't it be cool if they had manticores out here?" Kimi asked. "Or

Harpies? I'd love to see a Harpy."

"I don't wanna know," Carly grunted. "If I never see another weird monster with an animal head and a massive schlong, I'll die a happy woman!"

"Should we take a picture?" Garth suggested. "A memento of the time we captured and freed the Manotaur?"

"I want to forget that any of this ever happened," Carly groaned.

"And we didn't really capture him. More like clumsily guided him into wrecking a car and breaking a door," Amy said.

"And eating my jacket," Kimi sighed.

"All right, all right. But don't you guys wanna look back at some future point and remember, when you're old, that you once faced a great creature of myth in your own garage, and vanquished it in a great battle?"

The entire group stared at Garth without emotion. They let his words sink in, then looked to the creature on the back of the truck, gently snoring. Carly was the first to break the silence.

"I'm good."

"Yeah, me too," Amy said.

Kimi threw her hand up. "Well, I'm taking a picture. Me and Manny the Manotaur: BFF's forever."

"You can't be a BFF forever. The 'FF' already stands for that. That's like saying ATM machine," Garth protested, but Kimi replied by extending of a single digit of her hand. She grabbed her phone and snapped a few candid selfies, while the rest lingered around.

"C'mon, Car," Kimi said. "Come, take one with me."

"I'd rather eat—" Carly began. But before she could finish her sentence, Manny began to stir. He heaved his head up and slathered his tongue over Kimi's face and into her hair. She shrieked, while the rest jumped back, not wanting to be on the receiving end of another outburst. Lucky for them, the beast-man only jerked a bit before lying back down. But it was obvious to them all that the sleep-aids were wearing off.

"Get that tarp off him!" Garth snapped. The four leaped into action, untying the final knots and pulling the heavy tarp away.

Manny the Manotaur woke up not long after the removal of the tarp. He seemed confused as to where he was but didn't seem to mind to it. He jumped out from the back and began to sniff the grass. Only once did he look back at the four young adults whose house, garage, car, and day he had so violently wrecked. With a brief bellow and an angry grunt, Manny bolted off into the forest. For the first time, the group could see him move as he was meant to. Strong human arms grasping onto trees and the earth, while mighty hoofed feet pushed him forward. In less than a minute, he had vanished among the thicket of trees and bushes.

Kimi waved after the man-beast. "So long!" she said. "No hard feeling about

Garth's dad's car."

Amy and Garth waved along as well, both feeling a tad too self-conscious to say anything uplifting at the creature. "This is all very *Harry and the Hendersons*, isn't it?" Garth whispered in Amy's ear.

Kimi began to tear up. Despite everything the Manotaur had put them through, she couldn't help herself. Carly walked over and put her arm around her roommate, softly cradling her head against her shoulder.

"He's amazing, isn't he?" Kimi said.

"He sure is something," Carly admitted.

"Do you think, maybe, we could come over here from time to time? See if we can find him and feed him apples?"

"Oh, Kimi," Carly said, rubbing her finger through her friend's black hair. "Not on your fucking life." She then recoiled when she felt a thick glob of man-bull saliva sticking to her fingers.

"Well, back in the car, I guess," Garth said. "Did we decide where to eat yet?"

"Depends," Amy chuckled. "Are you hungry enough for Arby's yet?"

***

Three days passed since their adventure with Manny the Manotaur. Amy sat in the kitchen, sipping from her coffee and checking her emails. Ordinary life had returned to the house. For the most part, at least.

Carly and Garth were still trying to find out if their insurance would buy their story of having their car wrecked by a runaway bull. In the meantime, Garth was hiding from his dad, hoping to get the truck fixed long before he'd start asking questions about when he'd get it back. So despite some still unresolved issues, it was a typical quiet morning.

Thus, the greater Amy's surprise when she suddenly heard Carly roar in anger from the garage. Amy hurried outside, seeing her roommate running through the driveway in her pyjamas, swinging a tennis racquet wildly at three large birds. Birds with the heads and breasts of women. Women with razor-sharp teeth and Greek noses.

"Fucking harpies! Fucking harpies shat on my car!" Carly shrieked, as she smacked her racquet against one of the creatures. And to Amy's shock, she was right. The once red car, whose paint job had been scarred by the horns of Manny the Manotaur, was now near white from the copious amounts of Harpy shit.

To her surprise, a green circle of light began to form right beside the shit-stained Mustang. The light grew brighter and brighter, before vanishing in a flash, leaving in its place a fourth Harpy jumping and fluttering around, trying to get a grasp of this flying thing.

"Ah!" Amy said, having some questions from before cleared up, including the mystery of why their rent was so cheap.

Though for the few questions it answered, several more we raised.

"Amy! Do something!" Carly roared, as another Harpy ended up on the receiving end of her well-trained backhand.

"Guys!" Amy called out to the house. "Grab a net!"

"I'll get the sleep-aids," Kimi shouted.

RELENTLESS ARE OUR PURSUERS

By K.B. Elijah

So, I guess you're to be our dinner. Sorry and all that.

My eyes narrow on the deer, diverting from the gleaming intelligence in its eyes to the fat hunk of meat on its rear. I'm imagining it sizzling and spicy, roasted by fire and hot to the touch, the juices drizzling satisfyingly down my chin…

It will feed our whole family, I tell myself firmly, trying to ignore the delicate way the creature chews on the greenery, the scabbing cut on its ear that marks it as the survivor of a previous life-threatening encounter, the fact that at this time of year, it likely has a little one tucked away in a bush somewhere.

I swallow the thoughts, stamping down on them like one would a nest of ants. It's my turn to be responsible, my obligation to the family to do the hunting now that Da is gone, lost to the raiding orcs, and Ma is heavy with child.

Oh, doesn't that sound like a cliché?

That's me, little fourteen-year-old Eylem, living a storybook life of woe. Maybe my traumatised past will be swept away when it is dramatically revealed that I am the long-lost son of an ancient king with magic in my veins, destined to rule the lands and bring peace, as foretold by a prophetic oracle.

As if I'd leave Ma. Or Kat, or Jasparan. Even to be a prince.

I snort, and the deer startles.

Cursing myself, I force my limbs into stillness, barely daring to breathe. But the deer doesn't relax, and its ears continue to twitch, one delicate hoof poised in the air as if ready to flee at any moment.

I'm terrible at this. Not just bad—*terrible*. This is the first deer I've managed to get close to in over six hours, and I can't stay quiet enough to get it into a suitably relaxed state to take it down. Maybe I should try for a slow-moving dramada instead. Or a large log—that would be an appropriately matched opponent for my dismal hunting skills.

Movement to my right, a rustle in the undergrowth.

It's not much, but combined with my previous disturbance, it's enough to convince the deer to forage in another area of the woods. I watch the tasty lump of meat leap away to fill another hungry stomach.

"You scared it off," I say accusingly, ignoring my own contribution to that state of affairs as I turn and meet a pair of emerald eyes at a level just below my own.

But not only are they decidedly not amused at my undeniable attempt to shift blame, they're wide with fear and panic.

Kat crouches in the brush beside me, her breath coming out short and fast.

"Eylem," she hisses, a quiet urgency to her tone. "The orcs are here!"

I flinch, that famous instinctive fight-or-flight response having only ever triggered one thing in me when orcs are involved: cowering in a dark corner, preferably a deep underground cave, until they went away again. But that wasn't an option this time, not exposed in the middle of the woods as we were, not with—

Jasparan! My head whips around to where I left my brother, as if I could spot him through dozens of yards of thick undergrowth.

"This way." Kat slinks back the way she came, barely disturbing the bushes.

As for me? I step on three twigs, disturb a sleepy nest of dramada, who respond to my intrusion with angry chirps and indignant flicks of their tails, and stumble over something that was either a cunningly placed tripwire or just my own feet. Guess we'll never know.

"Eylem!" Jasparan calls out to me as we near, and I glance up from my scrutiny of the hazardous forest floor to find him curled into the base of a large tree, its shadows hiding most of his frail little body. A great hiding place, admittedly, but not where I left him.

"I told you both not to move!" I whisper, sharing the glare I shoot in Jas's direction with his twin. I know Kat was responsible for the disobedience; just as I know the sun rises over the mountains, orcs are to be avoided, and the red berries are the poisonous ones. Some things just *are*.

But now isn't the time for a full admonishment.

I turn to Kat. "Where are the orcs?"

She tilts her head to the east. "That way. I saw them as I was…checking on you."

That meant doing her own thing, despite my orders to stay put. But again, I let it go.

"How many?"

Her gaze falters. "Uh…"

"How many, Katsorias?"

"A dozen," she whispers, and my heart sinks. *A dozen.* We'd have been screwed if it was half of that, but a whole squadron?

"Eylem," Jasparan whimpers again, his little feet burrowing into the loose bistre dirt at the base of the tree. "I don't wanna get taken by the orcs." His words trail off into coughs, and I reach forward to pat his back, all too familiar with my brother's asthma.

"We're not going to," I say firmly, looking directly at him, and then Kat, making a promise that I know I may not be able to keep but would never, *ever*, let them know.

"We're going to get back to Ma, okay? And then we're all going to go so deep into the caves that the orcs will never find us, and we will only come out when we know they've gone. That sound okay to you, munchkin?"

Jasparan screws up his face, like he does whenever I call him that. I don't mind. It means he's distracted, not thinking about the orcs and what they could do…*would* do to us if they caught us.

For a moment, I wonder if heading back to the caves is actually the right thing to do, if we could be leading them to Ma. But then I almost fall over while I'm standing still not doing anything but thinking, and realise that I am not qualified to protect the twins from a bee sting, let alone a horde of bloodthirsty monsters.

I try not to panic, even though I have

no chuffing idea how to get us out of this. The orcs never come this far into the forest, ever, and I'm not prepared.

"We need to leave now. And we have to be quiet, okay?" I don't look at Kat. I'm sure she's rolling her eyes at my hypocritical words. "Jas, I want you to follow your sister and don't stop. No matter what happens, you keep *going*. You make it to Ma."

"That's your plan? Run for it and hope for the best?" Kat asks disbelievingly, and I don't like how unsteady her voice is, how much like a scared little girl she sounds. But that's all she is, really, just as Jasparan and I are two scared little boys. A group of terrified children without so much as a prayer to keep us safe from the orc's hands…or their cages, their blades, their whips…

I nod, not trusting my own voice with more than a single syllable. "Go!"

Jasparan uncurls from the tree, and I help him up, setting him down on the ground next to Kat as she takes off at a brisk walk.

Clever girl, I think, praising her silently as Jasparan and I follow. Running would give our position away, and if there's a chance that the orcs don't know we're here, we shouldn't squander it.

After all, it could mean the difference between life and death—

"Hell-oo? Anybody here?"

The voice echoes around the woods, seemingly omnidirectional in origin. All three of us freeze, a single statue of fear.

"No? No lost little cubs? Nobody here at *all*?"

The voice laughs, a cheery, good-natured laugh that might put anyone else in mind of fireside stories and home-cooked food. But we know better.

"Oh, come now. We can smell you. That stink of fear that your kind gives off, it wafts through these woods and leads us right to your door. Isn't that right, boys?"

A round of raucous jeers meets my ears, followed by a biting comment in a stentorian voice.

"And *girls*, you imbecilic oaf."

I didn't think it was possible to become any stiller than I was, but somehow I manage it, doing a fantastic impression of a lifeless rock.

That voice…her.

She's here?

No, she couldn't be. Akahfyr didn't go out on patrols, on hunting parties. She wouldn't be this far out. She barely left the orc camps at all, being far too important in status for such menial tasks.

I should know.

If Akahfyr is here, in these woods, it can only mean one thing. She's here for me.

I feel a pressure on my leg and let out a gasp.

But it's just Jasparan, tugging at me to move. Kat, ahead of him, gestures impatiently for us to follow.

They're right. We have to keep going.

The orcs are trying to distract us, to keep us rooted in place by fear.

And it's working.

I scowl at the feet that refuse to move, locked in place by the memories elicited by Akahfyr's voice. The nights of pain. Kept in a cage no bigger than myself, as the orcs guarding me took turns to poke burning pieces of wood through the bars. Being chained down and left alone for days at a time, crying out for food until they finally threw scraps at me. Amidst a circle of orcs with gleaming eyes and drawn blades, a circle which grew smaller and smaller until every one of them was within arm's reach of my exposed body, slashing and cutting until I fainted from blood loss.

And *she* was there for every single

torment I suffered. The first to land a blow and the last to call it off. I don't know what her fascination was with me, or how much better my life would have actually been if she hadn't been in it; one orc being just as cruel as the next. But Akahfyr was my fear, just as the Orc King had been Da's. Yet the King was dead—his death bringing the opportunity for our escape many years ago—and *she was here*.

"Eylem!" Kat risks using her voice to bring me back to the present, the barest of hushed whispers. Her green eyes are angry, and rightfully so.

I'm putting them in danger with my dilatory weakness. With the memories which Ma and I carry but the twins are blissfully ignorant of, born after our escape. They don't know what the orcs are like, other than what we've told them, but apparently that is enough.

Because my brave brother and sister are already fastidiously picking their way through the forest, several feet ahead of me, focusing on the goal and not the risk.

I can do the same. *Have* to do the same.

Taking a breath as deep as I dare, I lift one foot, and then another. And of course, as careful as I am trying to be, I step on the loudest chuffing stick in the whole chuffing forest.

Crack.

Its echoes dance around the trees like the streams of afternoon sun, mocking me. Mocking every care we'd ever taken not to be found; all the covering of tracks, the smothering of smoke, the twice-daily washes in the river to frustrate the orcs' enhanced sense of smell. Mocking Da's sacrifice last spring as he drew the orcs away from our cave so that we might continue to live free.

"We're coming for you."

The orc's voice is baked in satisfaction, as he pinpoints our location. But thanks to all of their yapping, I have theirs too: a few hundred yards to the south of us.

And that means we're going north.

"Scoot it!" I hiss at Jas and Kat, but they're already running, far cleverer than me.

Please, please, please, I beg silently as we race through the trees, dappled sunlight occasionally falling on Jasparan's back as he dutifully trails after his twin. *Please, no tripping, no catching up with us, no capturing, no killing. Not today.*

And for the briefest of moments, I have my wish, a spectacular few seconds where none of those terrible things happen and I dare to hope that we might make it.

But wishes are nothing but false hope followed by crushing disappointment, and this one fares no better than all of those which have come before. A flash of red ahead of us tells me all I need to know.

They have us surrounded.

"Left, Kat!" I call out, as loudly as I dare. "Down through the gorge!"

She changes direction without hesitation. Her feet sink into the soft mossy earth as she turns, with absolute faith in her brother's orders. I wish I had that same conviction, but the certainty of my instructions is nothing more than the desperation of running out of other options. The orcs are organised, militant in both their determination and strategies. We were miracles for having evaded them all these years, fools for thinking it could continue.

My breath pounds in my ears. We're running now, straining our bodies to go as fast as they can, noise be damned. The orcs are on our tail and they know it, the whoops and cries of a thrilling hunt puncturing our ears.

Relentless are our pursuers, their physiology made for chase and conflict, with thick hides, strong legs, and a stubbornness unmatched by any other creature in this world.

Except me, Ma always says. *Eylem, you could rival even an orc for pigheadedness.* She would tut fondly, swatting my ears whenever I acted up. But refusing to eat my greens is a far cry from the killers on our heels.

"Where are you running to, little children? You *know* you can't escape from us." The orcs' gleeful voices keep pace with us, tearing at our arms, tripping up our legs, the fear generated by their words turning into a palpable hurdle that actively resists our movements.

But we resist back, resolutely pushing through them like the thorny bushes at our ankles. Letting the words scratch deep but not take hold, knowing that to give in means a fate worse than death.

Jasparan coughs and stumbles, his little legs and lungs wearing out quickly. His voice is pained, scared, *lost*.

Kat glances back briefly, enough to see me grab her twin and swing him onto my back, before turning her focus back to herself. She's good, our Kat, better at moving through this forest than Jasparan and me combined.

But good may not be good enough.

There's a moment of panic as I realise that Jas is essentially now my shield, his body protecting my own from our pursuers, but it can't be helped, there's no other way but just putting one foot in front of the other, just keep going and not thinking about how heavy my brother is, just keep going, mind that rock there, duck under that tree here, so chuffing heavy, and I'm slowing, I can't slow, I have to keep going, watch that loose ground there, what the chuff have you been eating, Jasparan?—and keep going, and one more step, and another, and another, and I can't, and I *must*, and one more step—

One of my knees gives way, and I fall.

The heavy weight slides from my back with a whimper and another cough, and my face crashes painfully into a tree.

I've failed, I think, my entire life condensed to this crucial moment. *All you had to do was look after your brother and sister, and stay free from the orcs' rule. You've failed.*

But it doesn't quite ring true, as I catch sight of the sliver of wood above my head. An arrow, its fletching still quivering from impact, the barbed metal tip embedded an inch into the tree. The arrow has split the wood, the fresh raw whiteness of the tree's insides exposed to the world.

That could have been me. That could have been Jasparan. If I hadn't tripped—

But it's only a small and temporary blessing, because my fall has made us stationary and vulnerable, and then a second later the orcs are here, the flash of their yellowing teeth and red eyes and the bare steel of their blades surrounding us and the impaled tree.

We can't move. I can barely get to my feet by the time three spears find their way to my throat.

"Eylem," Jasparan whimpers from his position on the ground, as if I can get us out of this, as if one flick of my head could turn the orcs into harmless mush. I imagine there comes a time in every child's life when they realise that their big brother is not the hero they may have thought he was, but rather a useless mess who can't kill a deer to save his family's life and certainly can't outrun an orc.

Or a determined dramada, for that matter. And so if this is that moment for both Jasparan and Kat, *I'm really chuffing sorry,* I think, before I realise that no one is pointing any spears at my sister.

It abruptly hits me that she's not here, in this little circle of death that traps me and

Jasparan. Kat got out. She was fast enough to escape, and if none of the orcs know how many of us there are, have never seen Kat before now, maybe, maybe—

The moment is bittersweet. I helplessly watch as my brother bursts into fresh, wheezing tears, wetness running down from his golden eyes.

"Let him go," I plead desperately with the orcs. "I'll do anything. I'll come quietly. Just let him go!"

But if I had any expectation that the orcs had an ounce of mercy when they'd never shown it in the past, it quickly dispels like a burning log dropped into a lake when they simply just laugh at me. A very *wet* lake, if my metaphor wasn't clear enough. I can almost hear the sizzling of the extinguished flames of the last vestiges of my hope.

"Isn't he cute?" one orc sniggers, a chuckle in his throat. "Listen to his little whimpers."

"I'm not whimpering!" I yell, and they laugh harder. "You're just not listening to me!"

And then I remember, remember all the nights I spent shouting myself hoarse to no avail. All the times I begged, only to be ignored.

The orcs still hadn't learnt our language. They never bothered. Why would one study the tongue of pets and slaves?

I can understand theirs, born from years of listening and waiting. But neither

Ma nor I are able to speak it; our vocal chords and tongues incompatible with the guttural noises which form the essential core of the orcs' language.

It gives me a small amount of relief that Jasparan does not understand their verbal threats. Yet it makes an unbreachable barrier between us and the orcs, one that words will not penetrate.

"Jas," I whisper, turning my head as far as I dare with the cruel blades less than an inch from my throat. "I love you, okay? No matter what happens, I'm here."

Jasparan nods, his eyes still wet. His feet curl into the earth as if he can dig his way out, or hide until it is all over.

My heart breaks.

"Aw, look at them," one of the orcs

laughs. "Just a scared pair of cubs."

"Not nearly scared enough," Akahfyr says, and I flinch as she pushes her way to the front of the cluster of orcs.

Her scarlet eyes are just as my nightmares recall, cold and calculating, but with a flame of something else which is darker and more vicious. All orcs are cruel, but her presence seems to make the others seem dull in comparison, like blunt mallets compared to the wicked edge of a sword.

"Thought you'd run away from me, boy? I told you once what would happen if you ever tried."

I didn't just try, I think. *I succeeded. Thanks to Ma and Da, I've lived the last seven years of my life free of you.*

But none of that seems important when

she pulls the heavy chain from her belt, the endmost links still matted in blood and hair from whatever poor person or creature she last abused.

I can't breathe. I can feel the ghost of its stinging weight on my back, on my legs, across my head. The bloody nothingness it leads to, as she beats me senseless for some imagined infraction or merely because she's bored.

I can't help the breath I let out, a sharp hiss that divulges my fear.

"You remember this, do you, boy?" Akahfyr sounds pleased, and it is almost as if the last seven years never happened. I'm back in the orc camps, back in their cages, back working for *her*, catching, carrying, fetching, lifting...

"And what about you, little cub? Maybe we should teach you the same lessons as your kin."

Akahfyr lets the end of the chain drop to the ground, a heavy thump that promises pain and oblivion.

I close my eyes, trying to ready myself for the blow, but her words belatedly sink in. She wasn't talking to me.

Jasparan. *No.*

I don't care about the spears. I don't care about the chain. The only thing that matters in the whole chuffing world is my little brother, with his puppy dog eyes and happy laugh, his feet which are too big for him and the way he curls up to Ma at night as if he's still a baby. He's *mine*. Mine to protect, and if there's one thing I'm going to die doing, it's making sure my family is safe.

I leap for Jasparan, tackling him to the ground and tucking him underneath my weight. To my surprise, the spears pull away from us as I move, as if they're afraid we'll hurt ourselves.

No. They're afraid we'll *kill* ourselves, I realise. They want us alive—slaves are no use when they're dead.

But that protection doesn't extend to non-lethal blows, and I cry out as hot pain lances across my back from shoulder to hip. It burns in a way that fire never has.

"Naughty," Akahfyr tuts. She pulls the chain back for another lash, and I close my eyes, waiting for the impact.

I'm trying to think happy thoughts, I

really am, of the days we would spend chasing Da around the meadow until he finally slowed his steps and let us catch up to him, pretending we'd won. Of how Ma always tucked the best cuts of meat to the side for me, indulging my pickiness about fat and sinew. Kat's frustrated little scowl as her twin tried and failed to pronounce Katsorias when he was first learning to speak.

But the intrusion of darkness seeps into my mind regardless, less a memory and more the pressing sensation of fear and loss and failure.

I hold Jasparan tight beneath me, his small body warm and shaking, as if I believe I can actually protect him.

The second blow from Akahfyr hurts

worse than the first, a white hot slash of agony.

"Get them up," she orders the other orcs. "We'll drag them back to camp and teach them the cost of resisting us. I'll take a pound of flesh for every year that this one"—she gives my side a savage kick—"forced me to do my own work and carry my own supplies. You can have the runt."

A hand reaches for me.

Maybe this is the moment I should have given up. Thrown myself at Akahfyr's feet and tried to kiss her bloodstained boots as I'd seen other orcs do, in a universal gesture of submission. At the least I should have let them drag me away, in the hope that my compliance would garner me some good will.

But I've never been one for giving up. I spent six hours failing to hunt a deer just this morning and would have kept going until I'd obtained us all dinner, no matter how late the hour became. During our original escape from the orcs, Ma, Da and I spent eight days in the mountains without sleep, trekking through forests and across rivers and down steep rocky slopes that tore at our feet.

I also never lose staring contests. I think that says it all, really.

So maybe I should have surrendered, but instead, I decide that I'm going to fight to the chuffing end. There isn't a whole lot I can do, injured and surrounded, but when that hand touches my shoulder, I bite it.

My teeth sink into foul flesh, and I

almost gag, but the taste of the hand matters less than the satisfying scream of its owner.

"It *bit* me!" he howls, as if any person present couldn't see for themselves. "The audacity! Kill it!"

But I don't let go. I just bite down harder, shaking my head to tear at the repugnant flesh. And a moment later I'm rewarded with the heady sensation of the soft bones in his wrist giving way to me, folding their resistance into compliance as my jaw finds its way closed. There's a sudden loss of tension as the orc falls away from me, still howling.

I spit out the severed hand in disgust, the foul taste seeping into my mouth.

"You've done it now, boy." Akahfyr's voice is soft, and it sends more chills down my spine than if she'd shouted. "You'll be a bloody mess by the time I'm done with you."

I shut down the whimper that threatens to resolutely crawl its way up my throat. I made the choice to defy her, to keep fighting, and that choice is not a onetime thing. It's a creed, a lifestyle, a *commitment*.

And I am chuffing committed.

So no whimpering. Just an attempt at a menacing growl, and a sly glance at the hand curled in the dirt.

"Who's next?" I ask, with far more bravado than I feel. But this is better than being stuffed in a cage. If I go down, I go down with my head held high and my enemies' blood on my teeth, like my ancestors of old. Before our species were reduced to slavery and we lost the ability of flight.

Akahfyr's eyes glitter, the scarlet of her pupils making me bloody promises. There's a smudge of green in my vision as she raises the chain—

—and inexplicably drops it, her eyes widening. Her mouth opens, but there's no sound, just a flash of red that blossoms across her throat, and it doesn't make sense…why she's falling to the ground instead of standing straight—

There's a moment's silence as we absorb the image in front of us—a dead orc, my sister standing over her body.

Kat's claws are as crimson as my mouth.

"No one hurts my brothers," she snarls, whipping her tail above her head. She looks magnificent, a true representation of our species despite her small stature. Her scales glitter in the failing light of the day, putting my own dull colouring to shame.

I'm so proud of her, that for a long moment I'm struck speechless. She risked her own freedom to save us; she could have escaped without consequence. But for Kat, our dearest Katsorias, bravery comes far more easily than it does for me.

Jasparan wriggles out from underneath my feet.

"That's right!" he says, in his hoarse little voice, glowering at each of the orcs in turn. "Us dragons stick together, and my sister will kick your—"

He collapses into one of his coughing fits, and I obligingly tap him on the back, withdrawing my talons as to avoid accidentally puncturing his scales. The habit comes naturally, but it does hit me how absurd I must look, rubbing his back to ease his asthma when we are still surrounded by eleven orcs with weapons in their hands and murder in their eyes.

"I don't suppose we could call it even?" I ask hopefully, but of course they don't understand my words, maybe even misinterpreting my question as aggressive snarls. Kat's sudden appearance took them off guard, but they have quickly recovered, levelling their spears and raising their blades.

Jasparan gives a racking, heaving cough that, despite our situation, makes me turn to him in concern.

"Jas? Are you oka—"

A burst of fire erupts from his mouth, warm cobalt flames licking at our scales and inexplicably making me want to sneeze. But the orcs fare much worse, with their rough, greyish skin bearing no protection against fire.

Our brother writhes on the ground, claws scrabbling for purchase, as the jets of flame soar from his open mouth. The bark of the surrounding trees crackles, bubbling and blackening in moments, and I stare in horror as the effect is replicated on the orcs.

Their screams cut right through us, and I flinch, but our remaining enemies combust as quickly as the vegetation around us.

"How?" Kat asks, wide eyed and aporetic.

I've found my words again.

"Our amazing brother," I announce with glee, sweeping Jasparan up into my arms as the realisation sets in that all those bouts of asthma were anything but, "is a fire breather! We never have to fear the orcs again! He's a creature of legend! A myth in corporeal form! A god incarnate, the King of Dragons, the saviour of—"

The King of Dragons vomits on my shoulder.

"I'm hungry," Jasparan complains. "What's for dinner?"

FOREST OF MANY COLOURS

By Matthew M. Montelione

Marston marvelled at a forest of many colours. He relished the sunshine, breathing in the smell of fresh earth and basking in the thick, wet air. He smiled. It was truly paradise. "I've never felt stronger ground!" he said aloud.

"Why do you think that is, hm?" a raspy voice asked from behind him.

Marston flinched. He was alone in the woods. At least he thought he was. He turned.

A seven-foot plant with a bulbous head and teeth as sharp as pickets stared at him. "It is nourished daily by fresh blood. Come closer—I will show you!"

THE UGLY STEPSISTER

By McKenzie Richardson

The witch gave me a potion to make all of my ugly features disappear. All I had to do was swallow a drop each night before I went to sleep until I was satisfied.

The first morning, I woke up, and the

wart on my nose was gone. On the second, my sallow complexion had given way to a purer tone. Then went the age spots, the blemishes, the scars, the loose skin under my arms, the dark hairs on my knuckles. Each day, I woke up a little bit closer to perfection. Each day my longing for beauty grew and grew.

Because the changes were so gradual, I didn't really notice how much of me was disappearing. Looking back, I can't even really pinpoint what went first. Perhaps it started at my feet and worked up from there in a very systematic fashion. Or perhaps it was more sporadic–a fingernail here, an elbow there. Or maybe skin just disappeared inch by inch, a chessboard square at a time.

Regardless of how it happened, one day I woke up and when I looked in the mirror, all I saw was a pair of eyes, reddened with madness. I stared into what I had become, ever uglier in my feverish desire for beauty.

That night I took the last swig of potion and when I woke up… I was gone.

THE LAMPLIGHTER'S DEATH

By Olivia Arieti

Lisa shook off the icy shards from her coat, put on the apron, and headed towards the stove. The bundle of clothes she had to mend would wait. The men were about to come and needed to eat before thrusting themselves into the night. Life was tough for lamplighters; her father and brothers had to leave before dawn and twilight, whatever the weather or the season. The fellows were proud, though, and eager to pass the profession from father to son. It had become a sort of dynasty. Of course, their blood wasn't blue but grey, as grey as the mist that penetrated their skin.

The young seamstress had to work hard too, but didn't mind her hands red and pricked by the needle, for she had succeeded in ranking lots of the town's well-off ladies as her clients. In particular, she loved doing alterations for Lady Edith. The mansion was sumptuous, the servants friendly, and best of all, she would bump into Sir Gustave, the young and handsome heir. His wishful glances became her lusty torment. Like most of his peers, the gentleman claimed the right to the favours of every gorgeous inferior that frequented the household. Although disturbed by his conceitedness and arrogance, she often let her eyes meet his.

The consideration that she was doomed to a miserable existence due to her lowly origins was upsetting; nevertheless, she always managed to hide her unhappiness in front of the family.

Neither Dean, a timid newbie that her father had taken under his wing, ever noticed it. With worn-out clothes, ordinary features, and a gentle smile that masked the hungry grimace on his too emaciated face, the boy felt blessed to have been admitted to the group.

"Have a seat," said old Joe warmly, "Lisa makes the best stew in town." He cast a tender glance at his daughter.

Dean also gazed at her as though mesmerised by her good looks.

When the meal was over, just before leaving, he moved closed and uttered, "I'd like to see you again, Miss Lisa," and hurriedly walked out, almost ashamed of his advance.

No, she would never marry a lamplighter, there were enough in the family! Besides, the lure of a wealthy match kept crossing her mind. Could her beauty replace the lowly origins?

Perhaps she was too naïve at heart to desist from fairy tale dreams.

***

As time went by, Gustave appeared very infatuated, and the possibility of a proposal gained more consistence. Imagination replaced reason, and the ambitious seamstress already saw herself by his side. At nighttime, only doubts prevailed and turned into true obsessions. She had to find out about her fate! Her closest friend, Cecilia, suggested a visit to a medium.

The atmosphere was lugubrious as though the spirits were already hovering in the small room. Lisa held her breath in tremulous expectation while scrutinising the lady who, with semi-closed eyes, apparently had been transported into another world.

The slight flickering of the candle was the only response.

"It's too early, my dear," said the woman while collecting her savings. "You must visit me again."

Highly disappointed, the girl returned home, the unsolved question in her heart.

While Gustave seemed to take his time, Dean called frequently. Finally, Lisa acquiesced to have a stroll in the park with her devoted suitor.

However could she know that Gustave was taking a ride there with his mother?

Scorn and wrath flashed on his face. If

he could have descended the carriage, he would have beaten the boy.

Had she missed her chance if ever there was one?

Before taking leave, Dean kissed her hand, totally unaware of her agitation, and set forth to light once again what would never be enough to illuminate his beloved's darkness.

"Why didn't you tell me?" asked Gustave harshly the following afternoon when she was about to leave the mansion after collecting Lady Edith's gown.

"I had feelings for you and was beginning to consider the matter seriously."

He cleared his throat and added, "Naturally, mother would have never approved of such an union, lamplighters' daughters have never made it to aristocracy, but I would have challenged whatever to make you mine. It seems though, you prefer that squalid lad, a lamplighter I presume, as I have been told that you folks like to stick to your similar."

His words hurt her. They were sarcastic and unfair.

"Well, since you cannot be my wife, you may become my mistress, dear. I'm sure you'll enjoy it even more," he sneered. "Besides, it will make things easier for me; no need to displease mother at all."

After a quick glance that no servant was around, he took her in his arms and held her tight in order to feel and let her feel the heat of their bodies.

"Better get that creep out of your head,

love. I'm a jealous fellow, unwilling to share you with anyone."

Furious, Lisa ran out of the house, biting her lips and cursing her imbecility.

Thank goodness she had discovered just in time what a hideous bastard the gentleman was.

The flame of his embrace, the passion of the kiss, however, had kindled her senses and despite her anger, kept fuelling the heart.

Whether for despair or revenge, Lisa accepted Dean's courtship. Madly in love, the lad proposed a few months later.

The family was pleased and feasted the betrothal with jolly hearts, abundant ale, and a generous meal.

More than once, Gustave's carriage

passed before the couple and each time his glare fulminated the lovely bride-to-be.

The fellow ended up haunting her. His sarcastic remarks broke the nightly silence, while his rapacious eyes undressed her. The rabid touch on Lisa's virgin flesh was indelible.

"You want me, and you'll let me have you, sweetie," he whispered with the most alluring grin.

A perverse desire seized her. It was true—she wanted him.

***

It happened early one evening. The seamstress was about to go back home after delivering a new dress when Gustave got hold of her hand and dragged her into the library. The room was dark, as were the furniture and the leather couch in front of the fireplace, the flames the only flashes of light in such obscurity. Firmly, he pulled her towards him and uttered, "Whatever resistance would be vain, darling."

Then he delicately unbuttoned her blouse.

The sound of his voice made her quiver, and his hands running down her body kindled her with wantonness. Passion, true or untrue love, hate or scorn, all mingled in a medley of insatiable lust. The flames reddened even more before such unscrupulous ravishment and remained silent witnesses till their slow extinguishment.

"Now I *do* have the right to be jealous, my dear," he said as he showed her to the door.

The girl was devastated. The truth would have broken Dean's heart just as her refusal to marry him. Nobody would understand, and questions would become rumours. The following day, the wedding date was set.

The excitement of the preparations was not enough to dissipate Lisa's gloom. Her fiancé deserved much more than a sinful bride.

That evening the fog was thicker than ever and the cold bit as though famished. The men set out as usual. No clemency was tolerated; the lamps had to be lit. Nobody could explain how the tragedy occurred.

Probably, the ladder wasn't positioned correctly, or the steps were too slippery, or a sudden gust made it oscillate, and the young lamplighter fell and smashed his head.

Dismay and grief quickly replaced the mirth of the past days. The house had turned as grim and silent as its dwellers.

Tears of shame and guilt kept running down Lisa's face, a continuous flow of unspeakable regrets.

Gustave was now seen as a wicked fellow, so wicked as to nourish horrid thoughts and even more horrid suspicions.

Could he, blinded by jealousy, have been lurking nearby and pushed the ladder from the bar it was resting against, with the thick fog his accomplice?

Facing the villain would have been useless. He would simply mock her or consider her hysteric. Besides, she had no proof, and never could she let her affair with the depraved guy be known. The truth had to be sought, though, if only for her peace of mind.

If the living couldn't help, perhaps the dead would. The cadaverous medium flashed before her, but the result had been disappointing, and her last savings had been spent on the cloth for the bridal dress.

Once again, she sought advice from her friend, and the following evening Cecilia's spirit board was on the kitchen table. Dean certainly knew the truth. She wondered if he was too irate to answer.

The gusts hit the feeble panes as though

willing to force them open, and screeches and shrieks resounded all around. But Lisa couldn't afford to be afraid. No sooner her fingers had started moving the planchette than she shuddered; Dean was there.

That night Gustave pushed away the ladder from the post and made him fall. The spirit also had found out why and promised revenge.

The girl didn't dare to ask if he still cared for her; not even the love that had finally made its way through her shattered heart could dissipate such supernatural wrath.

***

Since Lisa stopped going to Lady Edith's house, one evening Gustave came to hers.

"Come, I have to talk to you, but I can't do it here. My carriage is outside."

Was he about to confess? The hope made her grab her coat and follow him.

The carriage moved away swiftly, as if in a great hurry.

"Where are we going?" she asked diffidently.

"Home, sweetheart. Mother is visiting her sister, and I was feeling lonely tonight."

"I thought you wanted to tell me something," she said with a challenging glare.

"I'm afraid there's nothing more to say except that I'm not sorry at all for your missed wedding. Haven't I made it clear enough that you belong to me?"

He looked at her lustfully before sneering. "Besides, you were too gorgeous for that insignificant bloke."

Fury seized her with such intensity that she opened the door and leapt out just when another carriage was passing by.

Only then Lisa realised that the unfortunate lamplighter still loved her; from then on, she would always be with him and spheres away from his perfidious rival.

INCARNATE

By Patrick Winters

Braxis sat on an oak stump, watching as his soldiers searched the remains of the village for valuables and food.

A hut burned at his back, keeping him warm against the chilled morning while he dipped his fingers into a pouch of cherries.

The general scooped out another handful and popped them into his mouth, one by one, chewing slowly. His fingers were still splattered with the blood of the slain, ruby-red droplets that were now half-frozen to the skin; it coated some of the cherries, but he didn't mind the flavour it brought to his tongue. A bitter tinge amidst a wash of sweetness—that suited him just fine.

The walls of the burning hut gave pleasant little pops and cracklings as he helped himself to another handful. A moment later, the frail beams holding up the blazing roof snapped, and the abode collapsed in on itself with a fiery *whoosh* and a flurry of embers, the dancing flakes of orange wafting over Braxis and the two men stationed at his side.

A woman screamed from somewhere nearby, and a panting old man rushed by in front of him, running straight into a pen of butchered pigs. One of Braxis's men followed at his heels, sword raised to cut off the chase, and more.

Braxis tongued at a morsel stuck in his teeth and glanced up to the grey sky. Crows were starting to gather here and there, circling about the rising pillars of smoke that spiralled up from the land, patiently waiting for a deathly meal. They would have their fill, thanks to Braxis and his men. And it was only too fitting, given what King Prine has said to him on the day their armies set out on their campaign:

Be kind to the carrion and no one else.

To this declaration, Braxis had dutifully—and readily—agreed, and it had given his army lease to raid and raze whatever came across their path. They'd already passed nine villages on their mission to conquer their neighbouring nation of Valonia. This meagre gathering of heathens made for the tenth. If any of the villages had names, Braxis did not know them. But then, he would not have bothered committing them to memory, if he had. They were small, rural places, with men who knew the toils of farming rather than the practice of war, and none had offered up much resistance or glory to his Croxian forces. Instead, they'd only provided brief flashes of play and slaughter, and, occasionally, needed provisions. This morning, Braxis and his men had only sought the former, as they were already amply stocked for their continued venture northward. He'd only bothered allowing his men to raid this paltry village because it was an expected benefit of conquest. He'd much prefer to be back on his horse and leading his soldiers onwards, making haste to the greater (and perhaps more battle-ready) populace of Brannon, which was to be their division's ultimate prize. The city was just another week's march away, and he was looking forward to a truer offering of conquest.

Once he'd finished the last of his cherries, Braxis rose. He wiped at his bloodied hands with the emptied pouch and tossed it aside, another scrap of refuse for the village's ruin.

He turned to the guards at his back. "We've had enough romping for now. It's time we return to real warfare." He nodded to one of the men. "You—go find Captains Orin and Glane. Tell them to start gathering up the men and make ready to march again. I want to be on our way before the crows touch down and take their first bites of what we've left them."

The soldier nodded and dashed off through a haze of smoke. The other followed at Braxis's side as they made their way to the edge of the village, where the rest of their forces and their steeds waited for them. They passed more burning huts and barns as they wound their way over the frosted earth, the Croxian soldiers putting torches to the lot of it and sticking swords through the heathen ilk that still drew breath. Those who didn't slay or burn darted about the ways, hauling along livestock that hadn't already been butchered. Others carried off what little bits of treasure poor folk such as this had owned. A few coins and baubles—but not much else.

"General Braxis!"

The call came from behind them. Braxis turned, peering about the smoky rush of things. He spotted a falconer, waving his arms about and dashing over bodies to reach them.

"General!" the soldier panted, coming to a halt and giving a bow.

"Speak."

"We've just received word from General Coltus." The falconer handed over a small roll of parchment. "His forces have seized the city of Eilos. Its ports are ours, and he says the remainder of the eastern coast is within our grasp."

Braxis unrolled the message and scanned it. Coltus's hand was small and his message lengthy—and no doubt quite braggadocious—but Braxis read just enough to confirm the falconer's words.

These tidings were to be celebrated. At this rate, the Croxian forces would have all of Valonia under their boot within two months' time. Perhaps even sooner, once his men claimed Brannon.

"Excellent." Braxis folded up the parchment and slipped it into his belt.

"Send word back to General Coltus of our progress. Tell him I'll reserve a brand new summer home for him in Brannon, should he ever tire of our Croxian winters…"

"Ah!" came a boisterous voice from nearby. "Now what have we here?"

Braxis turned and saw a pair of men pulling away at the crumbled walls of a paltry lean-to not ten feet off. As they hauled up a heap of broken boards, a young boy in ratty furs was revealed. He lay on the ground, sprawled across a woman; his face was buried in her bosom.

The boy looked up to the men that stood chuckling over him. There were tears on his thin cheeks, cutting paths down his soot-covered face. He might have seen ten years, if that; the woman, no doubt his mother, would see no more. Her head lolled upon her shoulders, eyes wide and unseeing, a wound in her belly and a line of red at the corner of her mouth.

"Another little Valonian pig for us to butcher," one of the lurking soldiers boomed. "Think this one will squeal, lads?"

The men that were gathering about the scene gave a round of affirmation. One of the soldiers made for the boy, grabbing him up by the arm and lifting his sword on high for one swift blow.

Braxi, with his eyes up to the circling carrion birds, shouted out, "Stay that sword, soldier!"

The expectant crowd fell to a sudden hush.

The soldier that had a hold of the boy nodded, albeit with clear disappointment, and shoved the child back down to the chilled earth. The boy let out a choked grunt as he fell back across the woman, and the soldier sheathed his sword. He stepped aside, eyes riveted to the ground in expectancy of a reprimand. But when Braxis spoke again, it was not to him, but to the whole of the crowd.

"This boy cries for what he has lost. He cries for his home. Friends. Family."

The general sauntered forward, taking casual strides over to the boy. He stopped and stood to the other side of the dead woman, then knelt down to one knee, coming eye to eye with the lad and sparing him a pitiful look. Braxis let his right hand hang over a burning piece of wood that lay at his side, the flame warming his skin and his ring, which was gifted to him on the day he became a general of Croxia. It bore the Sigil of Kyros, a symbol of their great god and his people's truest faith.

"He wishes to see them again and to be beside them in whatever afterlife his kind puts stock in. And we might give him that, with our blades and a quick thrust."

Braxis glanced to his men. Whatever measure of sympathy lay upon his face was there to mock. "But this," he bellowed, "would be a *kindness*."

He looked back at the boy, whose sorrow was steadily hardening into something more like hatred, his stare cutting daggers into the general. And that little show of anger made Braxis smirk.

"We will not kill him," he spat into the boy's face. "He will live to wander. To beg. And in the years to come, those he happens upon may question him of his hardships. When he answers them, and tells them that all the people of his village were killed save he, they may doubt him. They may think he exaggerates for sympathy and greater charity. So they will ask of him, 'How is it that your people were so very weak, to have all been slaughtered, as you claim? How could no more than you survive?'"

The general's hand shot out, grabbing the boy by the collar and tugging him up to his knees. As the boy hollered, Braxis brought his other hand up and pressed his now scalding ring into the flesh of the boy's cheek. The boy wailed in pain, and he threw fists and struggled to get away, to no avail, as his cheek sizzled beneath his tormentor's fist.

"But then they will see this brand—this symbol of our god, and our might—and they will know that against the forces of Croxia, there is *no defence*! And they will understand that he is no liar!"

His men gave a proud roar as he pulled his hand from the boy's cheek. He tugged the child here and there, getting a good look at his work, and was glad to see that the brand stood out stark and true, the Sigil of Kyros now burned into the boy's face for all his remaining years.

Braxis wrenched the boy back down, and the whimpering lad lay across his dead mother once again, rolling to and fro, cradling his cheek and screaming with a sorrowful fury.

Braxis rose back up and marched away, barking orders for all his men to hear. "Kill and burn whatever else remains in this forsaken village, and prepare to march on! Brannon awaits our arrival!"

His men gave another call for war and glory, and Braxis stomped off to find his horse and ready the ranks. As he went, he cast his thoughts up to the smoky winds and the cawing creatures that rode them.

Eat well, my feathered friends. Eat heartily.

***

Hours passed. But the staggering sorrow did not.

The boy lay beside his poor mother for quite some time, and he was still wallowing there long after the Croxian forces had disappeared into the northern woods.

He shook the arm of the woman who'd birthed him, and he whispered her name all the while, hoping a child's hope that these small acts alone could return her breath and her smile. He knew they could not; but he kept shaking and whispering, all the same, until he finally accepted her sad fate.

He eventually stood, suspended on quivering legs, and began to wander about the village. His steps were lethargic, his breaths were ragged, and his shoulders sagged further and further down with every corpse and flaming home he came across.

He called out now and again to whoever might hear him, but no answers ever came back. He could not find his father, search as he did, or his elder sister. The only faces to be found amidst the ruin were those of his neighbours and his youthful friends—or ones that were simply too bloodied and seared to recognise anymore. Crows came down to feast as he kept up the search, and no matter how he swore and shouted at them to go away, they would ignore him, or at best, flit aside only to seek out another of his forsaken people sprawled out nearby.

His branded cheek stung, the raw flesh aching with every step he took, but it seemed only a pricking thing compared to the great lamentation that carved away at his innards. It was a wicked thing, cutting and jabbing with every fond memory he recalled of this place, and it would twist its blade into his heart with every realisation that those memories—and everything and everyone that had helped to make them—now sat in a place of death and gathering ash. And that truth weighed on him, like a cold and soggy cloak.

When that weight became too much to bear, he fell to his knees, crying freely and fiercely before a young oak growing in the centre of the village, its branches now a halo of crackling flame.

He stayed like that for a fair while, crumpled beneath the heels of loss and sorrow. And when those horrid afflictions had hollowed him out through and through, another and much stronger emotion began to fill up the emptiness.

It started as a spark, striking to life as images of the cruel Croxian general returned to his mind's eye, along with the onslaught his men had wrought; but it quickly fanned into something far more destructive.

It was fury. Unholy and ferocious. The sort of rage that could shame the wildest tempest and bring the gods to shudder. And shudder they did, for the boy began to pray to them—to all the dark and vengeful gods his people had given name to and which Croxian ears had scarcely even heard of.

These deities heard the boy's prayers, and they sat alert on their thrones beyond the mortal world; as the boy continued to make his pleas and his vows to them, they could not but acquiesce.

The boy had asked them for revenge—and he would have it.

As he prayed, the air about the boy grew heavy with an unseen energy, flowing all about him while he gnashed his teeth and clenched his small fists. Then, that energy spread throughout the whole of the village. It went out in waves, crashing across the earth and kicking up clumps of frosted dirt, which began to collect into great earthen masses that floated about in the air like clouds. It caught the fires that blazed all around, and it lifted their flames higher, bending the element into living swirls and arches that writhed against the wind like great red worms. These fires darted from here to there—incinerating the feasting crows and sweeping up the bodies of the fallen villagers, eating away their flesh and carrying off their rattling bones as they whipped along.

The boy felt a similar fire rising up within himself; it grew, until his very flesh burned away, and his bared bones turned brittle, his mortal form turning to embers before his fiery eyes. But his rage remained true through the process, and the last scream he gave was not out of fear, or pain. It was for retribution.

And even though his body was reduced to ashes in the breeze, his heart remained, suspended in the air—blackened and charred, but still beating.

The elements and ruin of the village began to gather about the boy's heart, swirling around in a chaotic tornado. It all began to cluster and coalesce, creating a great mound of fire, bone, and earth. And from this mound, the gods moulded a new being, born from death and created out of destruction.

The creature was fury incarnate, and it roared at its existence.

***

The Croxian infantry marched on, eight abreast and with shields braced before them while the cavalry rode to either side of their lines, their long spears propped against the sides of their steeds. Great carts of gain and provisions brought up the rear, hauled along by the burliest of their horses. From on high, the sizable army looked like a river of gleaming metal, cutting straight through the Valonian forests and along the edge of the Barren Mountains, the lowest of the range's craggy heights beginning to rise up along their right flank.

General Braxis guided the flow of this warring river, leading his men onwards at a measured pace.

His loyal officers rode at his sides; they'd talked amongst themselves as they made their trek, speaking of battles past and matters at home, the morning's slaughter already cast to the dark backs of their minds. Braxis, however, remained quiet, keeping his eyes to the misty horizon ahead, though he listened in on what his men had to say.

Lieutenant Saffin, the youngest of his officers, was currently regaling them all with one of his many crude jokes.

"...but the whore, she's just not having it. So she says to the fellow, 'I already told you—*no more than three men at a time*!' So the fellow, he shakes his head, points at the scrawniest of his group, and says, 'But he's no man, my dear; he's a Talvanian!'"

The other officers let loose a round of guffaws, some giving joyful smacks across the young lieutenant's back. Even Braxis' stony countenance cracked a tad, a slight smile curling up at his lips.

"If you like that one, I should tell you about this maiden I knew in my boyhood," young Saffin said above the laughter of his comrades. "She had the most marvellous—"

In that instant, Braxis' ears perked and his head jerked about. He held a fist up and reined his horse to slow down.

"Silence!" he hissed over his shoulder.

His officers went as quiet as the dead, easing their own steeds in turn. They glanced about the trees to either side, listening for whatever had caught their general's attention.

There *was* a sound on the air—but whatever it was, they couldn't quite tell. It seemed as if it came from far off. But it was growing steadily louder. Closer. A kind of deep, roaring noise that repeated itself every few seconds.

"What in blazes is that?" Captain Orrin asked.

Captain Glane shrugged beside him, looking unconcerned. "A boar, perhaps? Or a mountain cat, up along the range? Some sort of animal. Sounds injured, to my ear."

Lieutenant Saffin shook his head, his eyes scanning the ridges up above. "Seems more angry, to mine."

Braxis thought much the same as the lieutenant, but as for a boar or cat? No. This noise was from something bigger. Much bigger. And as the sound grew ever louder, it seemed to him that it didn't come from the mountains, but from out in the forest.

Braxis looked back towards the trees on their left flank, looking past their carts and to the stretching path they had tread, waiting for another burst of noise to come. But instead, he heard something else: rapid rumbles, as though something enormous were running along the earth, and coming nearer to them.

A command to make ready formed at his lips—and then another roar rang in their ears, sounding out like thunder as some great, impossible creature leapt out of the forest, vaulting over the very treetops as it came crashing down into the midst of their ranks.

Metal crunched and soldiers screamed as the monstrous thing crushed Braxis's men beneath its colossal weight, kicking up dust and spurts of blood, and the general gawked at its unholy appearance.

It was some kind of hunchbacked golem to his eye, though he had never seen its like before. It stood nearly twenty feet tall, from stumpy foot to lumpy head, towering over his men as it let loose another of its bellowing cries. Its bulky and powerful frame seemed to be made from all manner of elements—a mass of human bones, wood, and earth, all moulded together and with some unnatural fire burning along its hefty limbs. And for whatever reason, it brought those limbs to bear against his men, swinging a tree-trunk sized arm up and walloping half a dozen men into the air.

"Spread out!" Braxis shouted over the din of combat and screams. He unsheathed his sword and nodded orders to his officers. "Get out from under it and away from its reach!"

But such orders were more easily said

than fulfilled, for the great monster let loose a barrage of quick fists upon his men, its club-like arms batting infantrymen aside or hammering them straight into the earth. The tearing of metal and the sound of the monster's rumbling squalls filled the day; the neighing of frightened horses joined the cacophony, though some cavalrymen were able to reign in their steeds and charge at the beast. Spears came stabbing up into the whirling monster's exposed sides, but if they did any good, Braxis could not tell. The beast simply kept moving and roaring, and when one of the cavalrymen came too close to it, it snatched up his horse by its hindquarters, lifted it on high, and brought man and steed smashing into another gathering of soldiers.

"Move back!" Braxis cried. But even as he said it, Captain Glane and Lieutenant Saffin advanced on the thing, and they were engulfed in a raging gush of flame that vomited forth from the monster's gaping mouth. They gave shrill cries of agony as the flames ate away at them, the fire already turning their armour to a molten mess.

Glane and his horse fell to the ground, each crushed beneath the monster's stomping feet, while the lieutenant's horse rushed off into the trees, carrying the screaming Saffin with it.

"Encircle the beast!" Braxis barked.

At the utterance, the raging monster spun about, pausing its onslaught to send a fiery-eyed glare straight at the General.

It let out another ferocious cry and leapt through the air, landing before Braxis and scooping him up in one giant hand as the general's horse bucked and fell to the ground.

Braxis hollered as the monster's grip tightened about the whole of his torso, his arms pinned tight in its clutches and its fire burning away at his cloak. Heat flooded through his armour and scalded his skin. And no matter how he thrashed, he couldn't escape the monster's hand.

The monster held him up, staring down at him with its cavernous eye sockets and those lantern-like pinpoints burning within them. Braxis continued to holler in pain and anger as it lifted its other hand up, extending one of its club-like fingers towards his face.

From out of its broad tip, a skeletal arm sprung forth, all bloodied and aflame with that unnatural fire, reaching out to him with a life it shouldn't have. Braxis tried to pull away from it, but it was no use.

The skeletal hand set its forefinger up to his cheek, its flaming touch branding him just below the eye and bringing forth a scream of torment. And as Braxis yelled, the monster's slack-jawed mouth rose up—into something of a smile.

After holding its touch for another moment more, the monster roared into Braxis' face, coughing up bits of dirt and flaky embers. Then it tossed him aside, launching him through the air like an arrow from a bow, the Croxian general tumbling head over foot as he sailed towards the distant hills of the Barren Mountains.

When Braxis crashed down, it was in a bruised and broken pile, his body lying on the edge of a high ridge. And while he was still breathing, he could not move—or feel—a solitary muscle. All he could do was lie there, his head lolling to the side, affording him a view of the utter decimation of his army occurring in the valley below.

The strange monster continued to roar and rage against his forces, until every one of Braxis's men lay splattered, crushed, or incinerated along the forest floor. The battle, such as it was, lasted for mere minutes; but to Braxis, the whole matter seemed interminable.

Finally, once all was said and done, the monster charged off into the trees, still letting out furious bellows that echoed on through the Valonian forests long after it had disappeared from sight.

Soon enough, crows came to feast upon the ruin of Braxis's army. The general had no choice but to watch this disgrace, for his life would not leave him—no matter how much he wished it to. And when the black birds finally came to eat of him, he still had not gone beyond the veil.

The crows ate well. They ate heartily.

INTANGIBLE

By Stacey Jaine McIntosh

She let the cold flow from within her, creating soft billowing clouds of snow as she walked. The frost bit at her lips; icicles formed in her hair and the cold clung to her skin. She breathed out, watching the tiny puffs of cold air dance before her frozen, blue lips. It was a spectacle as much as it was anything else. It was true, and he'd been right all along. She *was* the next Queen of Winter, and now it was time to take up her Staff and rule as only *she* could as *his* consort—the Summer King. She shivered, but not because of the cold—because of him—because of his warmth.

For as long as the fey could remember, Summer and Winter had been separate, never coming together as one, until now.

Beira smiled as she felt the heat he radiated, wash over her. It was a curious feeling, this mingling of temperatures, but not uncomfortable, like she had been expecting it would be.

"My Queen," Aodh said. "At last, I have been waiting for you."

Beira looked up at him, allowing her gaze to drift slowly over him. "So, I've heard."

She wouldn't fight him; to fight with a being such as he was pointless. The fey would always win, for they never played fair, despite their many rules.

She extended her hand for the Summer King to take. He kissed it, his lips warm and red against her pale and icy skin. Such a beautiful contrast; she found she couldn't look away.

Rule #1: Don't attract the attention of the fey. She had though, and this had been the price. She wasn't mortal, not anymore, but she wasn't quite fey either. Soon she would be. It was all a matter of timing.

Time was everything in Faerie; it was

also intangible, making it decidedly unimportant, not at all an easy concept to grasp given Beira's method of simple thought processing.

Rule #2: Don't insult them and never thank the fey. So far, she'd avoided that one, but she had no idea for how long.

The Summer King laughed, "Such beauty. It's simply breathtaking."

"Th—" She'd almost slipped up, but even still she knew that one mistake would cost her dearly. The Summer King, Aodh, wasn't known for his compassion or kindness, as was the way of most fey.

She offered him a smile instead, in compensation; he neither spoke nor moved.

Rule #3: Don't accept gifts from the fey. Little did Beira know that by accepting

Winter's Staff, she'd already accepted one of the most precious gifts a mortal could ever accept.

The Summer King smirked, as if reading her tortured mind, he said, "A gift like the one you hold in your hands was not given lightly, my Queen, do not disappoint or as surely as they," he paused and gestured with a wave of his hand to the fey that were now hesitantly crowding closer. "Will take it away, leaving you crumpled and destroying all that you once were."

"I u-understand, my King." There was a tremor in her voice that surprised her, and she hoped he wouldn't notice.

"You have naught to be afraid of Beira. Once the formalities of our union are out of the way, they will bow to your every whim, as has been the way of things since the beginning of time itself."

"But I thought the gifting of the Staff was—" *What else could there possibly be left for me to fulfil?*

"And it was, I speak of more private things, and what's a more fitting way to make you into my Queen than to take your maidenhood?"

Inside herself, Beira felt as cold as the snow and ice that swirled around her. Whatever the price, she must not insult him. She'd die otherwise.

She smiled and did not falter. "If that is what you desire, my King, then it shall be."

First published in Hawthorn and Ash, Iron Faerie Publishing, 2019

THE SHADES OF SYMPATHY

By T.M. Brown

Whatever sunlight once graced Sympathy had been suffocated by unrelenting grey clouds long ago. The once magnificent city was now a rotting corpse. Its winding, narrow streets were enveloped in perpetual gloom. Its grand plazas had become slick with mould. Its tumbledown residences gradually decayed amidst the stagnant mist. Even its towering, once proud citadel now bore the fruit of centuries of neglect. It was the dead capital of a dead kingdom in a dying land.

The city's crumbling skyline jutted from a sea of pale, white leaves like a dagger piercing the hide of some great beast. The whole forest was as still and silent as a grave. The eerie twilight that hung over the damned ruins was permanent and unchanging. The twisted trunks and branches of the ghostly trees now grew well into Sympathy's ruined streets. Whatever change occurred here was glacial. The Corpsewood slowly digested its unfortunate victim in uninterrupted solitude. The process would continue on for centuries.

Yet, from all death springs new life. Eurusal now had a new monarch—one which ruled its dark kingdom with an omnipotence even the wealthiest of Western lords would look upon with envy. An ancient, undying evil now held absolute dominion over these forsaken lands. Its leaching tentacles extended throughout these ruins. They likely threaded beneath the very ground the Sorcerer now tread.

Soňa Nediljka didn't want to be here. Indeed, she could scarcely imagine a more abysmal destination. She was well past her prime. Had circumstances been different, the Council would have no doubt selected a younger, more vigorous emissary. Under the current deteriorating conditions, however, the aging Sorcerer was all they felt they could spare. Despite her aching bones, her diminishing prowess, and her own personal misgivings, she intended to see the assignment through to its bitter end. She quietly feared it would be her last.

One who travelled to a place like Sympathy only did so with great purpose. Just as Eurusal had slowly been swallowed by shadow, so too was Soňa's homeland being swallowed by the rapacious Sunspring Empire. One by one, the independent kingdoms of the Shorn Coast had been coerced, bought, or conquered. The people of these lands languished under the heavy-handed rule of their new

Imperial Masters. Worse, the seers foretold of far more suffering to come. Soňa's great purpose was thus one of desperation—a final gambit to turn the tide of a losing war.

With every other conceivable hope exhausted, the venerable Sorcerer now found herself at the very edge of the world, seeking an alliance with the Old Parasite. Although she doubted any living person could make an honest claim to understand the creature's true power or motivations, Soňa accepted the gravity of her actions. Coming here at all was a gamble. She had served the Council of Vestril for all her life. If the creature found a way to manipulate her or turn her into one of its mindless thralls, the results for the already beleaguered kingdom could be disastrous.

To seek out such a loathsome creature was almost certainly madness. The folly of her quest became increasingly apparent with each passing day. She carried on nonetheless—an old dog too tired and too well conditioned to bite the hand of its master.

She'd prepared as best she could. Her mind was not only shielded by interwoven, abjurative wards of the highest calibre but was trapped as well. If the ancient creature tried to exploit her in any way, she'd be able to tear her consciousness into innumerable pieces. The ease of which it could be activated made the mind fragmentation spell a particularly dangerous enchantment. One could easily unravel their entire consciousness by simply tugging at a loose thread.

The ancient creature she sought out demanded such rigorous precautions, however. The few who spoke of the Old Parasite in these days of enlightenment were either stark raving mad or only did so in hushed tones after a few too many drinks. Some considered the creature to be one of Old Gods. Others claimed it was merely the hateful vestiges of a god who had long since faded away. A mad few contended that it was something even more primordial—an indifferent, primal being older than the world itself. All agreed, however, that the Old Parasite devoured entire civilisations and exploited the minds of those it consumed. As she approached the fallen capital of Eurusal, she no longer doubted the legends' veracity. She could feel the creature's hunger welling up inside her.

Under normal circumstances, the enchanted stones flitting about her would have illuminated an area the size of a cathedral hall, but the darkness here pressed close with unnatural tenacity. Pale, malformed creatures watched from just outside of her stones' dull glow. They skulked through the narrow streets and leered from the damp, stone husks of sagging shops and houses. They did nothing to impede her movement but eyed her hungrily from the shadows. Her mysterious guide's pace quickened as they approached the centre of the ruined city. The hooded man intermittently glanced back at her with cloudy, dead eyes.

The Splintered Citadel loomed before them. Its numerous, soaring spires were in a state of advanced decay. They would have collapsed long ago had it not been for the castle's current resident. Massive, gnarled roots twisted around the weathered granite, both suffocating and preserving a crumbling edifice that had long since lost the will to endure. Everything in this place was dictated in accordance with the Old Parasite's desires. The citadel remained standing because it willed the structure to exist. The twisted creatures that stalked her every move existed because it willed them to. Soňa arrived in this broken land alive and unharried because it had willed her to do so.

Her silent guide crossed a deteriorating drawbridge spanning a deep chasm. As she followed suit, she sensed an unsettling presence in the plumbless depths below. She knew better than to look down. The massive citadel gates ahead had been torn asunder by the relentless growth of blighted treeflesh. The path into the keep now stood open, obstructed only by scattered debris and sun-starved weeds. The baleful denizens of Sympathy gathered here in great numbers. They watched with milky eyes from atop the walls, behind arrow slits, and amongst the piles of debris. As she passed beneath the ruined portcullis, they glared down on her from the murder holes above. They crowded ever closer, pressing against the periphery of her muted light and preventing any withdrawal had she sought it.

Although the creatures' exact forms were difficult to divine in the pervasive darkness, it was nonetheless clear that they were cruel, grotesque mutations adapted to life in a world with neither sunlight nor the hope of redemption. Those she could not see, she could still hear. Hooked claws scraped at the floor around her. They descended the walls and clung to the ceilings. There were hundreds…maybe even thousands of them. As Soňa descended into the bowels of the castle, the Sorcerer found herself shadowed by a shifting horde of abominations.

She descended ever further beneath the Splintered Citadel. Each impossibly long, spiralling staircase was followed by yet another. Eventually, the stairs ended and her guide halted at a precipice overlooking inky black oblivion. He beckoned the Sorcerer forward but refused to join her. The throngs of vile creatures that had accompanied her since she arrived in Sympathy dispersed like rats before a slavering hound. Soňa continued into the darkness alone. The light of her stones struggled against the unnatural darkness. A hunched old man with a sallow face and milky white eyes hobbled out of the gloom. Deep beneath the Splintered Citadel, in the cavernous abyss, the old Sorcerer finally received the audience she had sought for so long.

"You've travelled far," the old man

commented in a passive tone. He leaned heavily on a gnarled wood staff.

"Indeed…" She paused. *This was it. Make or break.* "The Kingdoms of Veskir, Washalla, and Sentinel Stone beseech you to consider an alliance against the Sunspring Empire." Soňa's words were stilted and rehearsed. Had she not drilled them into her head during weeks of travel, she may very well have choked on them. The *creature* before her was not human. The old man may have appeared to be flesh and blood, but he was almost certainly not what he seemed. She could feel the creature's thoughts. It was the very embodiment of corruption and malicious intent.

"It's been a long time since we've

received such a request. You know…" the old man smiled through crooked teeth and pointed feebly into the darkness above. "The King of Eurusal once asked for similar assistance." He paused. "But you already knew that…" His cold eyes looked as if they could see right through her. She could feel the Old Parasite probing the wards that shielded her mind.

"So…will you assist us or not? We can offer you…" The old man didn't let her finish.

"It doesn't matter what you offer. We cannot assist you. Your time will come soon enough." Soňa's stomach sank. She understood at that very moment that she was unlikely to survive the encounter. There seemed little chance that this creature would be letting her leave if it stood nothing to gain from it. "I thought you humans had forsaken the Old Gods..." The old man stared expectantly at her.

"Whatever you are...you're no god. You're a disease...a pestilence." Soňa no longer bothered to choose her words carefully. The contempt emanating from this place was palpable. She could sense its intentions. She felt its pure malice wash over her. *Even if the parasite had accepted her offer, there could be no deal with such a creature that ended in anything but ruin. This entire journey had been a fool's errand.*

"Now is that anyway to speak with an ally?" The old man shook his head in disappointment. "Besides, you speak of things you can know nothing about." His expression softened to one of sympathy. "Oh, I know it's not your fault. You humans are the most cursed of all the beasts. You feel so strongly, scheme so quickly…yet, you waste away before you can accomplish anything."

"If you really have no interest in our assistance, then why did you permit me to come here?" Soňa could feel the parasite becoming more forceful in its reconnaissance of her mind. *She'd have to pull the thread before long.* The old man cast his gaze downward and shrugged his boney shoulders.

"We've always doubted that a human ever had the time to truly become bored… You wouldn't understand. We must wait for conditions beyond even our control. For now, we can only grant *your* ascendance, but rest assured…" The old man's gnarled staff began to grow from the ground. It rose higher and higher until it neared the edge of the suppressed glow around her. The old man dangled like a ragdoll from the rapidly extending tendril. His hollow, lifeless eyes stayed fixed on the Sorcerer while his mouth hung agape. A sonorous voice resonated—not from the old man, but from within her own mind. "You *all* eventually see things as they truly are."

The Old Parasite thrust itself into the Sorcerer's mind as quickly and violently as it had emerged from the earth. It tore through multiple interlocking wards simultaneously and with dizzying speed.

Soňa's consciousness, however, had been primed for disassembly. She pulled at the thread and everything began to unravel— her old home, her classmates, her family, the wars, the plagues, the good, and the bad. *She had failed in her quest, but she'd be damned if that creature would ever be able to use her against her own people.*

She could feel the very essence of her being slipping away. She clung to the knowledge that she'd done her best for Vestril and that, even if she'd failed her people, they would at least avoid the horrible fate that befell the citizens of Eurusal. Scenes from the Sorcerer's long life blurred and then faded entirely. *In just a few more moments, the damned parasite wouldn't be able to use her for much of anything.* Her memories were all shattered and then jumbled together like puzzle pieces. Soon she could no longer recall who she was or what she was doing. In a few more seconds her lungs would no longer remember to draw breath; her heart would not remember to beat. Consciousness began to fade from her, and she collapsed to the cold, damp ground.

Just as her breathing sputtered and her eyesight faded, the Old Parasite breached the last of her mental wards. It slithered its way into her rapidly collapsing mind. Just as it had stabilised the ruins of the Splintered Citadel, the ancient being halted the decay of Soňa Nediljka's mind. Her breathing steadied and her heartbeat stabilised. She stared blankly up at the lifeless body of an old man dangling from a great, twisted root like a child's finger puppet.

One by one, the Old Parasite began reassembling the shards of the Sorcerer's memory. The enchantment had been quite effective in rendering them unintelligible. An effort to reassemble them could easily take decades…perhaps even a century. The Old Parasite didn't mind, though. It liked puzzles…and it had plenty of time.

THE ORPHANED FAERY

By Zoey Xolton

The young faery knelt by her mother's body. She was still warm. She could almost be sleeping. Brushing golden strands of hair from her mother's eyes, Ashryn closed them with trembling fingers, before pausing to rest forehead to forehead—a final farewell.

Letting her tears flow freely, she carefully removed the crystal pendant from her mother's neck. Fastening it around her own, she held the precious crystal in her cupped hands. It pulsated with life, glowing in the gloom.

I will always be with you.

Her mother's voice echoed in her mind as her earthly body dissolved into the air…

First published in *Hawthorn and Ash*, Iron Faerie Publishing, 2019

ABOUT THE PUBLISHER

BLACK HARE PRESS is a small, independent publisher based in Melbourne, Australia.

Founded in 2018, our aim has always been to champion emerging authors from all around the globe and offer opportunities for them to participate in speculative fiction and horror short story anthologies.

Connect

Website: *www.blackharepress.com*

Twitter: *@BlackHarePress*